Lucas
and the
Freighter

Malania E. Reynolds

THREE SKILLET

Lucas and the Freighter

 THREE SKILLET

www.ThreeSkilletPublishing.com

Cover typesetting and formatting by Farley Dunn

ISBN: 978-1-943189-48-9

— 1 —

Sarah Griswold disembarked from the *Liberty Belle* at the Port of St. Louis and stood to the side as the other passengers came down the ramp. The bright sun overhead provided little heat. Along the riverbank, two cows stood with their ankles wrapped in mud, as they pulled at grass along the water's edge. One lifted its head and let out a mournful sound that jerked up at the end before it dropped its head, took several heavy steps away from the water's edge, and found a larger clump of greenery to munch. Sarah wore a full-figured, dark green silk dress of the latest style from New Orleans and a hat trimmed with an ostrich feather, with a veil over her face. She carried a black lace parasol in her left hand and held the hand of a boy about five years of age with her right hand. The boy tried to point to the animals, but the lady pressed his hand to his side without any indication she saw them. He looked at her with apprehension, and she moved closer to the building to get out of the cool, dank-smelling air. She seemed to be waiting for someone and gazed toward the town.

An open wagon waited on the street, with two mules nibbling out of feed bags hanging from their necks. Their tails twitched, but they seemed well trained and content. A second wagon rumbled by, pulled by four horses and laden with newly offloaded goods from the ship. Several enclosed carriages disappeared into the city, their occupants unobserved and isolated from all around them.

Watching Sarah from a short distance down the wooden wharf, a tall, lank man of uncertain age hunkered in the shade. He was dressed in the plaid flannel shirt and faded blue trousers of a muleskinner and mountain man. The britches had a thin yellow stripe down the outside of each leg indicating they had once belonged to a soldier. A black, shiny vest covered his chest, while his brown wool coat hung on his shoulders, a size too large. He had a beaver cap on his head and high-topped boots on his feet. A holster sporting a side arm was at his right elbow, and a leather scabbard held a long, thin-bladed skinning knife. The man shifted position, and in that moment, it seemed he could use the weapons with equal precision, if required.

Sarah slowly became aware of the rugged man's presence. She glanced his direction, then let her eyes jerk away, tracing the buildings disappearing into the distance. The streets were dusty with the wheels of wagons, and along the raised wooden boardwalks, various people could be seen. A woman twirled a parasol while a girl in a matching outfit skipped at her side, eating treats from a bag, and dropping as many as she consumed. Two men in dark suit jackets over stripped trousers carried on a conversation that became animated as she watched. A skinny dog appeared from an alley, trailing the girl and the woman, hungrily snapping up the treats along the boardwalk. After a while, the newly disembarked passenger holding the boy's hand glanced back at the man in the beaver cap, and seeing his eyes still on her, she turned away nervously. With determination in her steps, she gracefully walked to the ticket agent's window. The other passengers had long since gone their way, and the platform was deserted except for her, the boy and the man.

"Sir, please excuse me. Is there a cheap hotel near the station where I might eat a meal and refresh myself?" She spoke with the soft, pleasant cadence of a Southern lady, and the man watching her came to full attention.

"Sure, ma'am. The Webster's Plymouth House is about a mile away, to the north of Frontier Street." The agent wore a green shade positioned over his eyes and held a pencil in his hand. A pair of bright red garters wrapped around the sleeves of his brown shirt. He gave a quick smile. "Left my grandmother in Alabama when I decided to come west to seek my fortune. Don't know

7

that I ever found the fortune, but your voice brings back my memories of her. Anything else I can help you with?"

"How would I get to this hotel? Is there a public conveyance that we might ride?" She didn't comment on the man's reminiscence about his relations. She looked sideways, only to shift closer to the ticket window when she saw the beaver cap still haunting the shadows, with his eyes looking her direction.

"Nope. Ain't no public conveyance that I heerd about, but that man over there has a freight wagon." The man scratched his head with the flat end of his pencil. "Maybe he'd give you a ride into town." He pointed his pencil at the man dressed in the beaver cap, and he called loudly, "Hey, Angus, you headed back to town, soon? This lady and her boy need a ride to the Plymouth House." He turned to Sarah. "Best I know he can get you there, ma'am. He works for the United States Army. You can trust him."

Sarah looked at the boy, still tightly gripped in her hand, and looked as though she might protest, but before she could form a response, Angus stepped to the window to stand beside her.

"Did you call to me, Casey?"

The boy's eyes darted from face to face, taking in the expressions of the man behind the counter, the beaver-capped man, and Sarah. His interest revealed an alert and watchful mind; a good sign in a young boy.

"Shore I did, Angus. Have you suddenly gone deef? The lady wants a ride to the Plymouth House.

Tell Plano while you're there, his package has come on the boat from New Orleans." He dropped his pencil on the floor and stooped to pick it up, calling out to no one, "Bother my britches. Cain't hang onto one of these for the life of my sainted grandmother."

Angus faced the woman and removed the cap off his head. A scar ran down the side of his scalp, about three inches long, leaving his hair parted in a zigzag manner. Sarah let out a gasp, before tilting her head down and watching the boards at her feet. If Angus was offended, he didn't show it. "Hello, ma'am. I can offer you transportation to the hotel, if you don't mind riding along in a freight wagon."

"I could hardly impose." The breeze from the waterfront shifted her veil, revealing a strong chin and a nervous smile. The feather in her hat fluttered with gusto. After a pause, she asked, "Are you certain you don't mind?"

Angus Meldrick held his cap in his hands, and he winked at the boy. "I had no intention of stopping at the hotel on my way out of town, but seeing as you and the boy need a ride, I can hardly do otherwise, for such a fine young man, standing so silent and still by your side. Reminds me of my own son."

"You have a child?" Sarah's stance softened with the question.

"Lost in the influenza epidemic that took Mary, his wife." Casey had his pencil firmly back in his hand, and he worked at a sheet of paper totaling the anticipated profits or loss from the disembarked steamship.

9

He didn't look up to see Angus glare at him for the unasked-for remark.

"Where's your luggage?" Angus could barely see the light of her eyes under her heavy veil. She was clearly uncertain whether to speak to a stranger, or ride with him the mile to the hotel.

"My luggage?" Sarah looked around before finding a small trunk about twenty feet away where it had been unloaded by the stevedores from the steamboat. The trunk was rounded on top and tied with two ropes to keep it secure. Beside the trunk were several wooden crates. On the side of three of the boxes, in bold letters, were the words Jefferson Barracks, Missouri Territory. She pointed to it with her parasol. "There, I believe. You're an Army man?"

"Yes'm. Like Casey said, you can trust me. Name's Angus Meldrick." He nodded at her respectfully and pointed to the words on the boxes. "You headed to the Barracks, ma'am? So am I. Why don't I lift these onto my wagon, and I'll take you to the hotel?"

"If you would be so kind." She leaned to the boy and touched his face, saying, "Be patient, Lucas. We'll be on our way soon. We've someone to help us." The boy glanced at Angus and offered him an embarrassed smile.

Angus replaced his cap and made his way to the wagon, clasping one mule by the flanks and rubbing it for a moment before leading the animals along the wharf to stop beside the offloaded luggage. He swung the trunk into the wagon and went back for the crates.

On the floor, almost hidden until he had moved the boxes, were two large carpetbags, one of faded blue, maroon, red, and tan, and the other predominately green, yellow and white. He lifted them into the wagon and started to grab the lone box still on the pier when Sarah stopped him. It was of a larger size and marked differently from the rest.

"That one isn't mine, sir." Her voice was low and sharp.

He left the box and walked to the agent's window. "Heh, Casey, does this crate belong to Plano? I can take it to the hotel, since I'm going there, anyway."

The ticket agent put his head to the bars so he could see the one box left on the wharf.

"Yeah, that's the one for Plano. I'd be grateful if you'd take it to him. Then I can go get my dinner sooner. When you going to the Barracks?"

"Soon's I can get there. You finished with my paperwork, yet? I'm off when I get this woman's things settled on the wagon."

"Just about." Casey pulled a sheet of paper from a hidden stack, added it to several already in front of him, and marked several items on it as he talked. "I heard there was a brawl down at Slim's saloon last week, and a couple of men was killed, one of them a soldier boy. The sheriff was saying they fought over Lily, but Tom Lafferty said it was about a card game. You heard anything?"

"Nah, I just came up last night from the south to pick up the supplies." He glanced at the woman. She

11

was whispering something to the boy.

The agent pushed a pile of folded papers at him. "Here's your inventory sheets. I heard someone say they're getting ready at the Barracks to ride down to Santa Fe. You going with them, when they go?"

Angus took the papers and stuffed them into his coat pocket. "I suppose I will. Either me or Claymore. I don't fancy driving all that way; but that's what I get paid for. I'll see you soon, Casey." He turned, picked up the final box, flung it onto the back of the wagon and tied the flap of the burlap cover down. He walked to the woman and boy.

"I'm ready to go, ma'am." He swung the boy up to the seat of the wagon and took the lady's arm. He breathed deeply and smiled as she moved past him. She carried a small, maroon-colored velvet bag with a long brass chain for a handle; it swung back and hit him on the cheek as he helped her to climb up the wheel and onto the seat. He raised his hand to his face but said nothing.

He removed the feed bags from the mules' necks and dropped them in the rear of the wagon, then went around the vehicle and climbed to the driver's seat, let go the brake, and the mules started moving. Nothing was said on the way to the hotel. He guided the mules around the traffic in the street, clicking his tongue at them and occasionally calling a direction. They presented quite a picture, a lady dressed in silk going to the Barracks, possibly the wife of an officer, and a driver as rough as they came. No one seemed to pay them much mind, however, as many of those around them were as mismatched or worse.

He pulled up to the hitching rail and swung down from the wagon.

"You stay here, ma'am, and I'll take Plano's box to him and ask about a room. What's your name?"

"Sarah Griswold."

"Griswold." He stopped short when she said it. "Any relation to Adam Griswold?"

"You know him?" She smiled underneath her veil and tucked the boy's hand into her embrace.

"Perhaps I do." He untied the cover from the wagon and lifted the crate from the back. He carried it into the hotel lobby and set it on the floor next to the desk. Once inside, he called, "Plano!" A short, portly man came through the curtain behind the counter.

"Howdy, Angus. Are you staying in town tonight? I got a room at the back empty, if you want it."

"Let me think on it. I have a box from Casey. He said to bring it to you."

"Thank you." The clerk came around and studied the box on the floor for a moment. He smiled, satisfied. "It must be the books I ordered. I buy them by the weight, not by author or title, from the warehouse in New Orleans. Save a lot of money that way, but I have to take what they send. Anything to read is welcome, I say." He knelt to lift the box, but Angus stopped him.

"What was the name of that soldier killed in that brawl last week involving Lily the saloon girl? Do you know?" Angus frowned like he was trying to solve a riddle.

"Sure, Adam Griswold. Thought you might have heard, already. It's about, everywhere."

"Just got back in and don't know nothing. Think I might have someone outside who knew him. What else you know?" Angus lifted his cap with one hand and rubbed his scalp with the other. He closed his eyes and shook his head.

Plano was at the box, opening one corner. He looked up. "The other guy's name was Langston. He was a civilian. Why are you asking? You must have heard about it at the Barracks." He pulled out one book, scratched his head and frowned.

"Yeh, that's what I thought his name was. I think I have his relative in the wagon outside. Come here." He led the clerk to the window but stayed far enough back that the woman couldn't see them through the glass. "See? She just came up from New Orleans; dressed real fancy in silk. Got off the steamer, and her luggage says Jefferson Barracks. She wants a room to freshen up. She said her name's Sarah Griswold. You let her have that room of mine you offered, and I'll park the wagon at the livery until I find out what's happening. Is the sheriff in town?"

"Why, yes. He's at the restaurant eating his dinner, I think. I saw him walk down that way. Do you think this woman's Griswold's wife?" He stared at the pair sitting in the wagon.

"I don't think she could be; she must be more than ten years older than Griswold; but that's an unusual

14

name. Well, I best be getting out to her; or she'll be suspicious. You keep quiet until I talk to the sheriff. If she don't have the money, I'll pay you."

He walked outside and stepped to the wagon.

"He's got a room at the back, ma'am. You come down, and I'll see you settled." He helped her over the side and smiled again as he caught her fragrance. He held his arms wide, and the boy jumped into them. "You go in, and I'll bring in your luggage. If you're going to the Barracks tomorrow, I'll come back for you."

He lifted the trunk from the wagon, carried it into the lobby and set it down near the back wall. He went back for the crates and carpetbags. He saw her at the counter talking to Plano Jeffreys. He returned to his wagon and drove it to the livery, where he asked if he could park it until he returned for it. He paid the man for shelter and hay for the mules, then left the livery and walked toward the Hash House; it wasn't the best restaurant in town, but cheap enough.

The bell above the door to the restaurant jangled a welcome. The smell of fried onions assailed his senses, and he wrinkled his nose. His stomach growled in sympathy. He saw Wade Terrill, the sheriff, in a corner flirting with Majesty, the waitress. He walked toward him and spoke in a respectful tone. "Good afternoon, Sheriff."

The sheriff nodded his direction.

Angus didn't wait for an invitation, but sat down in the chair across from him. "Give me some eggs and ham, Majesty, please. I'm hungry enough to eat my mules, feet first." She laughed and went to place the order in the kitchen.

"Howdy, Angus. Glad to have you sit down and join me." The sheriff looked at him inquiringly. "I don't suppose you'd be here sitting at my table if it wasn't important. We know each other well."

"Yeah, well, not that well." Angus ducked his head, and his neck glowed pink.

"No?" The sheriff smiled. "I remember a few times you've gotten some drunken private out of jail with your own money, rather than have him taken to the Barracks to be disciplined by the army."

"That? Common courtesy. Anybody with the sense of a thick-skulled heifer would do the same." Angus looked around to see if his voice could be overheard and stopped when Majesty brought him a cup and filled it full. He leaned forward when she left the table. "Sheriff, I think I've got a problem on my hands."

"A problem? From you? Well, dang my ornery soul to tarnation. You just yanked the rug out from under me, man. I never expected that from you." The sheriff had taken a sip of coffee; he swallowed and gaped at the freighter. "What sort of doings have you managed to wrangle your way?"

"I think the wife or mother of that lieutenant killed in last week's brawl in Slim's saloon has shown up on the steamer from New Orleans this morning, and I don't know what to do with her." He kept his voice low, although there was no one who could overhear

16

him.

"What? Good God, man, what are you saying? Griswold's wife is here?" The sheriff looked around him, as if she might be present in the room.

"She's at the hotel." Angus cleared his throat and ducked his head, and he took a sidestep. "I could be wrong, as she seems too old for a wife, so maybe some other relative, but she definitely said her name's Griswold. I mentioned Adam's name, and she asked me if I knew him."

"Angus, you fool!" Wade slapped the tabletop, causing Angus' coffee cup to rattle on its saucer. "You told the woman the man was dead?"

"Now hold on, Wade. I did no such thing." Angus puffed up, upset the man would think such a thing. "I just told her I might know a man by that name. I told Plano to keep quiet, but you know what an old gossip he is. She's bound to hear something soon. I was waiting for Casey to finish the papers on the freight that came on the boat, so I could take them to the Major, and she was standing there with a little boy, apparently thinking someone was coming to fetch her. The print on her luggage said Jefferson Barracks, plain as the sun was shining, and she said her name's the same as his. Of course, I asked her about it. Who wouldn't? Then I got to thinking, maybe that's why the lieutenant was in town, to meet her. And get this, she's got that boy with her, about five, or thereabouts. I been trying to place whether the man had a kid, but I cain't remember none such." Angus ran out of words and leaned back, while Majesty set his plate before him and poured more coffee for him and the sheriff. She looked between them with a lifted brow, but when the two men remained silent, she left them alone.

"Holy Mother of God, this sure puts a different slant on the whole thing." The sheriff spoke in a hushed and intense tone. "I thought it was odd that he was involved in that brawl. The witnesses contradicted each other. The sergeant said that he was an innocent bystander, minding his own business when the fight started. Judge Maddock was there, and he said the man who died, a civilian named Todd Langston, accused Garland of cheating on the roulette wheel. Garland said he didn't know anything was happening until he heard the shots. Of course, he would. I don't trust that gambler, but there's nothing I can hang the accusation on with so many telling different versions. It's certain he was the one who fired his weapon; his pistol was still hot. Griswold got caught in the crossfire, looked like to me. The Army said they'd take care of the body and see it had a decent burial." He looked up when the bell jangled.

Angus looked around, his fork suspended full of egg, halfway to his mouth. He saw the graceful, full-figured form of Sarah Griswold come in with her boy. He couldn't help the break in his voice.

"That's her, Wade, and the boy. Mrs. Griswold. They must have come for food. I don't know when they serve the last meal on the boat, but the boy must be hungry."

"See to her, man," Wade said. "Maybe we can unwind this tangle and get the matter sorted. Go." He motioned with his hand, finally rapping the table to get Angus to move.

Angus pushed his chair back, sending the legs scraping across the hard floor. As he stood, Sarah Griswold looked his direction, and the boy waved at the familiar face. She grasped his arm, and with a quiet admonition, she forced it to his side. She began to search for an empty table. Angus strode toward the woman, waving to Majesty to come forward. His back had grown damp with perspiration, even though it wasn't overly warm.

"Mrs. Griswold, won't you sit with us? Is everything well at the hotel?"

She nodded and followed him to the table. He pulled out a chair, and she sat down with a sigh. He helped the boy sit next to her.

"Ma'am, Mrs. Griswold, this is Sheriff Wade Terrill. He wants a word with you." Angus picked up his fork and stared at his cold eggs and ham. His coffee had grown lukewarm and no longer steamed in the still air of the restaurant, as the tableau unfolded around him. He motioned to Majesty and held up his coffee cup.

The sheriff looked up when Majesty appeared to take Sarah's order. She spoke politely, ordering ham and eggs with milk for the boy. When told they only had canned milk, she agreed that was fine. She looked at Angus with a question in her eyes, but he looked at

Majesty as she poured him a fresh cup of coffee. His face was pink with embarrassment, and when Majesty stepped away, he looked to the sheriff rather than towards Sarah.

"I'm pleased to meet you, Mrs. Griswold. Our business can wait until you eat. What's the boy's name?" Wade leaned back in his chair and frowned at Angus for putting him in this spot. With the fresh coffee to restore the order of his meal, the freighter grinned back at him and took a sip of his coffee.

"Lucas. We call him Lucas. What do you want to talk to me about? Now's as good a time as any to speak of it." She looked from one man to the other. The only sound was from the boy, a bumping noise that was shaking the tabletop. She glanced at him and told him to quit kicking the table leg. Majesty poured her a cup of coffee and went back to the kitchen. The bell jangled again, breaking the continuing silence, and two ladies came in, Pearl Quigsby and Margaret Smart. They looked like they had been shopping, for they laid some packages on the floor beside their chairs.

Wade Terrill groaned; he muttered aside to Angus, "Of all the townspeople to frequent the restaurant at this time of day, it has to be the two biggest gossips in town."

"Pardon, did you address me?" Sarah smiled politely, although she must have been edgy from hunger. She could barely keep her eyes off the food on the table, and the boy was watching the remains of Angus' plate with more intensity than was seemly.

"It'll wait, ma'am. Did you come on the boat from New Orleans? Angus here said he took you to the hotel. I trust you found the accommodations satisfactory." He stopped when Majesty placed her plate in front of her and a smaller plate for the boy.

Sarah reached to take off the veil and hat so she could eat, exposing hair streaked with gray, with beautiful eyes, gray with long dark lashes. She laid the hat on the edge of the table near the salt cellar and sugar bowl.

"Yes, thank you. The hotel's adequate. I've come all the way from Natchez; and I hoped to go on to Jefferson Barracks today. My nephew wrote that he would meet me at the ticket agent's, but he didn't come. I suppose he's busy with his soldiering work." She looked at Angus with a question. He shook his head.

"What's your nephew's name?" The sheriff glanced at the two women now ordering their meal. He spoke softly and turned to give Sarah his full attention when the two women didn't seem to be listening to his conversation.

"Adam Griswold. He's a lieutenant in the First Dragoons, G Company." She caught Angus' eyes squarely, asking, "Do you know him? Earlier you mentioned his name, so I assume you must." She turned from Angus and began cutting the ham into small bites for the boy.

"I don't have much association with the officers, ma'am, though I do overhear their names at times."

21

Angus spoke nervously. He glanced at the sheriff, who nodded at him to keep talking. "I drive the freight wagon of supplies, and sometimes I scout ahead if we're on the move, or carry dispatches from one fort to another. I'm a civilian contractor, work for myself, although I get paid by the Army. How did you like Natchez? Were you there long? I was there once a few years ago."

The door opened again, and a group of men came in. It was becoming clear that they would get no opportunity to speak to the woman privately in the restaurant. Angus looked at Wade, who seemed to have realized the same thing. He was concentrating so hard on the men who had entered that he started when she answered his questions.

"I lived in Natchez for some time. My aunt and uncle lived there, but they died in the scarlet fever epidemic a few years ago. My cousin sold their home on Black Bayou, and there's no one left there for me to claim as my own." She leaned closer and swallowed a sip of coffee. "My niece died last month, and I've come to bring Adam's son to him. I had no choice but to write to Adam, as I have five children of my own to care for." She wiped the boy's mouth of grease from the ham and helped him to some milk. The boy grimaced at the taste of the canned milk.

"I see," said the sheriff. "And, is your home in Mississippi?"

"No. We have a small farm north of Mobile, in Alabama. My grandmother was a Creek Indian; and

I've left my husband and the children with servants to bring the boy. Adam was at Fort Mitchell during the trouble in 1836, and he met and married my niece Parabella there when my father was taken prisoner because of an altercation at the fort. He was released, and the major portion of the tribe was sent north to Fort Gibson in Kansas Territory, what is now called Oklahoma. I was sent, along with my mother, to Natchez, to live with my aunt and uncle, since we were considered white. My mother died there, and I married my Samuel, Adam's uncle." She finished her meal and sat back in the chair. She donned her hat and lowered her veil, carefully placing it over her face and touching her hair to make sure it was smooth. The motion brought to Angus' attention the back of her pale pink neck.

The sheriff cleared his throat and looked hard at Angus. The man looked back at him. They each shook their heads in dismay.

"Is this what it's about? Has Adam told the authorities that I'm part Indian?" She looked defiant, and the sheriff quickly tried to reassure her.

"No. No. It has nothing to do with that. I'm heading to my office. Angus will bring you there where we can talk in private." Wade rose, tipped his hat and went to pay his bill. He spoke to Majesty, and she smiled.

"Would the boy like to go outside for a minute? I'll take him, Mrs. Griswold." Angus pushed his empty plate aside and placed his folded napkin beside it. His coffee cup was empty, and he set it upside down on the plate.

Sarah looked at him with a puzzled frown, and she became aware of the boy squirming in his seat. She nodded with a grateful smile. She remained at the table as Angus picked up his cap, paid for his meal and left with the boy. She sat a few minutes before approaching Majesty, only to find Angus had paid for their meal. She gathered her things, left the restaurant and waited in the chair on the porch for Angus and Lucas to return.

Several clouds graced the sky, providing shade over sections of the street, and giving a measure of coolness to those who happened along. In the distance, Sarah observed three men discussing and studying the undercarriage of a wagon. One of the men wore formal clothing, a brown coat with lighter lapels, pale pants, and well-made shoes. The other two were rougher, dressed as livery men, in stained clothing. One of those with the livery wear dropped to the ground and climbed underneath. The other two leaned down at the waist and watched, pointing from time to time. After a time, Sarah turned away as Angus and Lucas appeared from beside the building. Lucas was skipping along beside the much taller man, and he reached down to pick up a rock. Angus smiled and waited for him.

"What'd you find, Lucas?" Angus called to the boy. When he caught sight of Sarah waiting on the porch, his body jerked in surprise.

"It's a rock." The boy showed it to Angus, who turned his attention from the woman and looked at it carefully, as though it were a nugget of gold.

"That's a fine rock, boy. What'll you do with it?" He looked at the child, to see him put it in his pocket and race to his aunt.

Angus stepped on the porch, laughed and tipped his hat. "Ma'am?"

"Thank you for paying for our meal. I didn't expect that, and I appreciate your kindness." She stood, gently straightening her skirts, and placing the end of her parasol on the wooden porch floorboards. It tapped once, with a solid clunk. "I believe Mr. Terrill wished to speak with me in a more private location. Will you take me to him, now?"

"Certainly. Wade, er, Sheriff Terrill is at his office. It's just down the way a bit. I can walk you there." He offered her his arm, and they stepped off the porch.

"Lucas?" Sarah called to the boy. "Come along. Either stay at my side, or you'll need to hold my hand."

"Yes'm." He chirped his answer in a bright, only marginally interested voice, but he appeared at her side. He had the rock out again, studying it as they walked.

"He's a good child," Sarah remarked to Angus, in a conversational tone. "He's been very little trouble on the trip. He does like a bit of mischief now and again, but a firm word usually brings him along. I'm certain my nephew will have no trouble with him, being Army. It's a shame the boy's mother is no longer alive. That's what he really needs, a strong maternal figure. What's done is done, however, and Adam will have to fill in the gaps best as he can."

Angus let her talk without response, but his face spoke to his answer. His expression grew distressed when she remarked about the dead man taking care of the child. He didn't seem to notice when a large horse pulling an enclosed carriage rumbled alongside them, stirring dust from the street. Instead, he pointed to indicate the entrance onto the boardwalk. Helping Sarah up as she lifted her hem to keep it unsoiled, and waiting on Lucas to join them, they strode to the sheriff's office. He opened the door, and the noxious odor of unwashed bodies assailed them. Sarah pulled a kerchief from her purse and held it to her nose. He helped her to a chair and retired to stand against the wall. The boy whispered something to his aunt. She glanced at Angus and nodded her head. Lucas joined Angus, standing in a similar fashion.

"Yes, Lucas?" Angus looked at him with a raised brow.

"Aunt Sarah says I can wait with you, if you're of a mind to let me."

"Long as you're not rowdy." Angus winked.

"Thank you, sir. Can I sit?"

"If you think the floor'll do."

Angus smiled when the child dropped to the wooden floor, with his legs spread wide, and began rolling his stone across the boards from one side to the other. The sheriff, who had been looking at some papers on his desk when they entered, finally rose and sat back down.

"Mrs. Griswold, am I correct when I say that your

husband is the uncle of Adam Griswold of the Dragoons? A lieutenant, I think you said?" The sheriff looked very serious, and he spoke his words with an even clip. It was as though he was speaking a rehearsed speech from behind a formal lectern at a legal proceeding.

"Yes. That's correct. He's been at Jefferson Barracks for six months." The boy remained on the floor by the door. He seemed disinterested in the conversation. He lifted the rock and examined it with exaggerated scrutiny.

"I'm sorry, but I'm afraid I have bad news. Adam Griswold was killed last week, Wednesday, that is, during a fight in a local saloon. The major took the body to Jefferson for burial, since he was an officer."

"Killed?" she croaked. "My nephew was killed?" She turned to Angus. "You knew this, and you didn't tell me?" She rose, walked across the room and slapped him on the face. Angus blinked hard. She was breathing fast and her eyes were fierce and angry.

"Now, Mrs. Griswold. There's no need for violence. Angus had nothing to do with this. He was away on a trip to pick up supplies. Please control yourself. You'll upset the boy." Indeed, Lucas had jumped up and run to his great-aunt and was buried in her generous skirt. He looked frightened.

"You could have told me," she accused Angus.

He shrugged and called to the boy, "Come with me. Your aunt and the sheriff have matters to discuss. Let's see if we can find you a matching rock. Then you'll have one for each pocket."

Sarah looked at Lucas, hesitating for a moment, then she disengaged his arms from her clothing and pushed him Angus' direction. "Go ahead. You know this man, and he'll watch out for you."

Angus picked up the boy and exited the office to wait outside, leaving the sheriff to unfold the details of the lieutenant's demise and burial.

Angus leaned against the porch post as Lucas jumped down both steps in one bound. The clouds had filled in the sky just overhead, and the street was in full shade. Dust flew at the boy's feet, and he laughed. He squatted to study the shadows under the elevated walk, and reaching underneath, he pulled out a rock. He held it up to show Angus.

"You got a quick eye, boy." Angus nodded at him approvingly. "Bring it up here so's we can compare it with the other one. Did you bring it outside with you?"

"Yessir." The boy fished in his pocket for a moment, before pulling out the first stone. He held them both in one hand, offering them up to Angus. The clouds overhead shifted, and the sun washed the scene, causing the second rock to sparkle.

"Got some mica in that new one. See the sparkles?"

He and the boy sat in chairs on the porch and watched the traffic move slowly down Main Street, as they traded the rocks back and forth, discussing the peculiarities of each. After a while, Sarah Griswold and the sheriff came out. Her eyes were red-rimmed and puffy from the shock of learning that her nephew had been killed during a fight in the saloon.

"Angus, take Mrs. Griswold to the hotel for now. If you can stay with her and the boy and drive them to the Barracks tomorrow, when she's calmer, see that she talks to the major or someone in authority in the Army. There's nothing more I can do. It's their responsibility. I'll see if I can get more information out of the civilian witnesses, but the Army's in charge of the investigation into the lieutenant's death."

"Very well, Sheriff Terrill. Come on, ma'am, I'll walk you to the hotel." He took her arm, and she didn't resist. They made their way to the hotel, and he opened the door for her and the boy. She marched up the stairs without saying anything, the boy clinging to her hand. He heard the upstairs door close and turned to Plano, the clerk.

"What room did you put her in, Plano? Two-fifteen? Watch out for her; she's had a shock. She's the aunt of the lieutenant who was killed in Slim's bar last Wednesday. See that she has whatever she or the boy needs, and put it on my bill." He took out a silver coin and placed it on the counter. The metal ping of the coin sounded so final. "I'll be at the livery with my wagon and mules for a while; I plan to see the barber while I'm here. Maybe, I'll take a bath while I'm in town." He put his nose under his arm and made a face. He groaned.

"She's the lieutenant's aunt? The one who was in the fight over Lily, the prostitute? What did the sheriff say?" The clerk was clearly hoping for something juicy to spread around the town. It was none of his business, although the news wouldn't stay hidden long.

"Yes. She's the lieutenant's aunt, and the boy is Griswold's son. Came to be with him 'cause his ma died, and he has no place else to go, apparently."

"Might be a few men in town interested in a real lady." The clerk snickered suggestively, and he picked up the extra room key, to toss it in the air and catch it again.

"I don't think so, Plano. I'll be back to check in on her. Let me have that extra key." He held out his hand. "I'll look in later and see how she's doing. You keep this under your hat, Plano. She's a real lady." He watched the clerk nod in understanding, although he carried a gleam of mischievousness in his eyes.

Angus spent most of the afternoon at the livery, grooming his mules and sledging grease onto the axles of his wagon. He talked with Jasper, the livery man, and within an hour, one of the town merchants stopped by the livery to tell them the news that the deceased lieutenant's aunt and son were in town. Angus eventually made his way to the town's lone barber shop where he had a shave and his hair trimmed. He took a bath in the shack in back of the place, taking care of much of his accumulated filth and smell, although he had to put on the same dirty clothes. He cursed himself for not having gone to the store and bought a new shirt and trousers. He remedied that situation and changed into the new clothes in the back room. He also bought a red neckerchief, although it was a color he normally wouldn't have chosen. There was a brown felt hat on a rack, and he paid for it, too. He threw his oily, smelly beaver cap in the dung heap out back. He'd acquired some extra money in a poker game at the Barracks and could afford to splurge on new clothing. It was getting late by the lengthening shadows from the storefronts. He put his soiled clothing in the wagon, to be washed by a woman at the Barracks who needed the extra funds.

He went to a Mexican restaurant he liked and chose some beans, chili and corn meal cakes. He washed them down with a beer. Then he had another. When he came out, it was dark. He walked back to the sheriff's office, but Wade had nothing else to say, so he went to the hotel. Plano told him the woman was still in her room, so he sat on the porch and waited for her to come out for dinner.

The town was coming alive for the night. He could see from his vantage point on the hotel porch that several riders were in from the local ranches, and just on time, the stage coach stopped at the station. Only one man got off and walked up the street. Angus couldn't see where he went and let his eyes rove the street for other action. He paused on the saloon where the boy's father had died. There was no action there, as the authorities were taking care of the investigation, and it had long ago moved on from the saloon.

"The major will know," he mumbled, now sleepy. "He'll be able to tell me more tomorrow when I get to the Barracks." He stood and headed to check on the woman and the boy. The lobby was quiet, and Plano was gone to eat his dinner. He'd been replaced by James Volker, the night clerk. He waved at the man as he crossed to the stairs.

Angus knocked softly, and when there was no answer, he cautiously opened the door with the key he'd rescued from Plano and saw the woman standing at the window, her silhouette clear against the brightness of the lights from the streetlamp. She held a handkerchief to her eyes, which were red-rimmed and shiny from her tears. The boy was asleep on the bed.

"Hello, Mrs. Griswold, I'm just here to see if you're coming down to supper."

"No, I'm not hungry." She walked toward him with an angry look in her eyes. She held out her hand. "I'll have the key, please."

There was nothing he could do. He handed her the extra key and went out the door.

— 2 —

With a moan of discomfort, Angus crawled from his temporary bed between sacks of grain in the back room of Foley's Mercantile and Grain. He massaged his back and glared at the hard floor on which he had slept. He hurriedly dressed and left the room. Foley was just coming in the front of his store.

"Mornin', Angus. Sleep well?" He guffawed and tossed his key in the air. He was middle-aged, with a mustache that resembled corn silk. He was dressed in a dark suit, white shirt and string tie that dangled past his vest.

"I've slept in worse places, but at the moment I can't think where. Thanks, Foley; tell the missus I hope she feels better today."

"I'll do that. Heh, that woman what came in with the boy; Garrison said she's the aunt of that lieutenant

33

who was killed in Slim's place. You taking her out to the Barracks?"

"I have that intention." Angus put his hat on his head, prepared to leave.

"I've got a package for the major, came in on last night's stage. Could you take it to him?"

"Sure, I'll take it. Where is it?"

Foley went behind his counter and pulled a brown paper package from underneath it. "Came from Chicago, must be important." He handed the wrapped package to Angus, who grasped it with both hands to find it was heavy.

"Dang, Foley. Warn me first." Angus let out a huff of air.

"Heh, a strong man like you? Didn't think you'd have trouble carrying that." Foley laughed. "I wondered why the major ordered it through me, 'stead of the regular Army dispatch, but I don't ask questions. You just give it to him."

Angus lifted an eyebrow, tipped his hat and left the store. He walked to the livery, threw the package into the back with his supplies and hitched his mules. One of them was acting out and tried to escape, but he gave him a whack on the nose, and the mule lined up with his twin. He left them waiting while he, the woman and boy ate a hasty breakfast. She wouldn't look him in the eyes and seemed subdued.

They were on the road early and arrived at the barracks by noon. He commented on the busy activity, but the woman ignored him. The boy was gazing around, his eyes wide with curiosity. He left the wagon near the supply depot for the quartermaster's assistants to unload and walked with Mrs. Griswold and the boy to the officers' quarters. Sergeant Pomeroy was behind the desk, and he told him why he needed to see the major. Angus explained quietly that he wasn't really involved in the legal process but felt the woman needed the support of someone who knew her. They didn't wait long.

"Ah, Mrs. Griswold, come in. I'm sorry to have to be the bearer of bad tidings. Sit down, please." Cletus Johnston, the major in command at the Barracks, looked at Angus as though to ask why he was there but didn't challenge him. The two men had a strong bond that went back many years to when Angus had first started working with the Army as a young man. The major had tried to get him to join and become a member of the armed military, but he'd refused. However, he'd followed him from Fort Leavenworth when the major had been reassigned to the new post.

"Major," Angus said, to break the moment. He worked his new hat in his hands absently.

"Angus, I'm glad to see you back. How was your trip?"

"I've had better. Got a package from Foley for you in the wagon. I told Private Murphy to take it to your quarters. Left the supplies with the quartermaster." There was a question in the muleskinner's eyes.

The major looked at him askance but didn't satisfy his curiosity over the package, just nodded. He saw the boy and called, "Sergeant!"

"Yes, Sir?" The sergeant poked his head in the crack in the door.

"Why don't you take the lad and show him the puppies in the bakery? Come back in about thirty minutes." The boy looked at his aunt, his eyes bright and clear. She nodded, and he went meekly with the sergeant.

"Major, Mrs. Griswold has spoken to Sheriff Terrill and gotten the general news from the civilian side. She needs to know what the military have discovered about the fight in the saloon."

"Well, I've scheduled an inquest for Friday, but I don't think we'll learn more than is already known. It seems that the man named Langston accused Garland the roulette dealer of cheating, and Garland pulled his gun and shot Langston. We're not certain of how your nephew was involved. The witnesses disagree on the facts. One says he was caught in the crossfire as Langston pulled his gun to defend himself, and one witness says Griswold started it over a saloon girl named Lily."

Sarah paled, and she clenched her hand at her chest.

"Begging your pardon, ma'am. That's what they said. I sent Captain Tennant to investigate and bring the body back for burial. He had a really nice funeral, ma'am. The whole company was there." He looked up when she pulled her handkerchief from her handbag, the same one she had used the day before, and wiped the tears from her eyes. "I tend to believe Judge

Maddock and my sergeant, who saw the whole thing. He's an honest man. The gambler Garland has disappeared. The Army has no jurisdiction over him since he's a civilian. I think the best thing is just to wait until Sheriff Terrill or someone finds the man and brings him to court."

"That's all? You're going to let the man get away with killing my nephew? He's given more than a dozen years to the Army, and this is the thanks he gets?" She screamed at him, and the major stood to face her.

"Settle down, my dear. I know this has been a great shock to you, but these things take time. And, since there were two men killed, one of them a civilian, we must let the civilian law officials work out the details of it. It was on civilian property, not a military post; so they have the first priority. I assure you, justice will be done; it just takes time."

She sat down, pressing her kerchief to her face, and the major sat, too. He adjusted the sleeves of his jacket unnecessarily before looking up. He wore a tight smile.

Sara continued, more in control, "What about this woman, Lily? Have they talked to her? I know my nephew wouldn't be with her when he knew that I was on my way to him. I got a letter from him at the first of the month with the money for my fare. He made all the arrangements for me to join him here with the boy. He said he'd be at the steamboat pier to meet me. He wanted the boy to live with him." She gulped and swallowed, tears in her eyes. She used the handkerchief to wipe them away.

"As for the woman, Mrs. Griswold, there's nothing solid to charge your nephew with about that. Simply a rumor. The captain and Judge Maddock saw nothing to indicate that the lieutenant knew the woman. He asked for a week's leave of absence and received it from his company commander. He was apparently making arrangements for you to stay in the town. He didn't talk to the quartermaster about rooms on the post. He had spoken to Mrs. Mattie Lake about renting a room in town at her boarding house, Captain Tennant discovered. I'm sure, if you talk to her, she'll let you and the boy stay there. We don't have accommodations for civilians on the post."

"I don't have the funds to stay in town. I only have a few dollars left from the money he sent for my meals and the boy. I must get back to my husband and family. I only came to bring the boy. What'll happen to him?" Her big eyes began to swim in tears again, and she brought her handkerchief up to dab at them. The major looked to Angus, but he only shrugged.

"Well, as to that. I can have you fill out the forms, of course, for some sort of trust for the boy, but we can't keep him here. I don't have any hope that you'll receive anything, because the lieutenant wasn't killed in the line of duty, sort of like. On civilian property, and by a gambler? I don't think they'll agree. You can try; that's all I know what to tell you."

"What'll I do, Major? I have my own family to raise. My husband doesn't want the boy." She wailed and cried.

Angus interrupted the proceedings. "I'll take care of the boy until other arrangements can be made, Mrs. Griswold. I don't have much besides my salary with the Army, but I have a place here where he'll be safe and get plenty to eat." He gulped and glanced at the major, who looked at him as though he'd never seen him before.

"What're you saying, Angus? You barely make enough to take care of yourself, much less a small boy. You have only two rooms near the blacksmith's shop. Why, it's not practical." The major tried to dissuade him from his offer, but the woman seemed to think it was a splendid notion.

"Oh, Mr. Meldrick, thank you so much. I'll be ever so grateful." She smiled and stood as though her business was finished.

Angus left the boy in the charge of Sergeant Pomeroy, with the major's permission, and showed the lady his quarters near the blacksmith's shop. She held her handkerchief to her nose at the smells coming from the corral where several mules and horses stood waiting to be shod.

He lifted her green, yellow and white carpetbag into the wagon and was soon on his way back to the town with the woman, now all smiles and bubbling over with talk of her family in Alabama. Angus wore a dazed expression and played the part of a delivery man with another package to transport, for that was his job.

He stopped at the hotel and helped her down, and took her bag into the lobby, where Plano was standing behind the counter, his eyes wide with curiosity. With scarcely a word of farewell, the woman walked up the stairs and disappeared into the same room she had occupied the night before.

"What's going on, Angus? Where's the boy?" Plano pushed his eye glasses higher on his nose.

"He's at the Barracks." He sighed. "She said she can't keep him."

"Who's going to keep him, then?"

"I am," he said with resolution. He reached into his pocket and drew out a lone silver coin, gazing at it with regret. He laid it on the counter. "That's all I got left. You see that she gets to the boat pier. If she needs more money; you talk to Sheriff Terrill. My appreciation, Plano."

Outside, he untied the reins and climbed aboard the wagon seat. Clucking to the mules, he pulled away from the hotel porch and drove away, his hat flapping in the strong breeze from the south. A bird landed a few feet in front of the path, and the mules shied away, but he held a tight grip on the reins, his concentration on his driving.

— 3 —

Angus and the boy set up housekeeping in his two rooms next to the blacksmith's shop. The front room consisted of a couple of chairs, a table, two lanterns that hung from pegs on the wall, a moldy horsehair sofa, and one huge fireplace with a box to store the kindling. The back room held a bed, a table, a single ladderback chair, a small shelf for his comb and brush set and shaving mug. There was a cloth rug on the floor some previous woman had laboriously made and several pegs on the wall to hang their clothing.

The small trunk was filled with the boy's clothes and extra shoes. He emptied it and left the trunk on the front stoop. He found a watertight canvas tent and hung it over the trunk to keep out the rain, placing the pole and stakes behind it. The crates were emptied of their contents, which happened to be books and dishes. He dismantled the wooden crates to be used for firewood.

The dishes were set on the only shelf provided near the fireplace, bringing a somewhat more cheerful atmosphere to the rooms, and he found a long flat board and stacked the books on top and beneath it along the base of the back wall. Someone had sent the remains of the mother's possessions to the boy's father, perhaps thinking he would find them useful. Angus had found a cast-off tea kettle at some Army post in the past. He made a cup of tea and offered it to the boy, but he refused to drink. Since there were no provisions for civilian contractors to have extra rations, they ate their evening meal in the dining room with the raw recruits and the disciplined old-timers in the last years of their enlistments. Only two women ate in the mess room with their husbands, one named Florene Walters, and Jenny Skidmore, the laundress. Angus spoke to both women, asking if they had interest in adopting the boy, but neither were prepared to take on an orphaned child.

The water keg was between their rooms and the blacksmith's shop and held rainwater. The first thing Angus did after returning from the depot was to fill a bucket of water from the horse trough at the black-smith's shop and scrub the walls and the floor of the rooms. They settled down, and he went about his work, leaving the boy for long hours and sometimes days alone to brood or walk along the boardwalk from one end of the fort to the other. The officers' wives looked at him askance, and he stared back. He sulked and brooded, and Angus couldn't find a way to entertain him when they were in the room alone. He tried a board game played with marbles, but the boy took the marbles and rolled them across the floorboards, instead.

Their first quarrel came as a surprise. The night had started pleasantly enough, with dinner in the mess hall and a sweet desert of spice cake. Lucas asked to take his portion back to their room, to eat later, and the cook offered him a small piece of brown paper, with which Angus wrapped it and carried it to their quarters. He carelessly laid the package on the table, some worse for the wear from their walk across the compound. Telling Lucas to ready himself for the evening, Angus took one of the books from the shelf and started reading while the boy prepared for bed. After several minutes, Lucas let out a wail, and his eyes turned red as he gazed at the smashed contents in the wrapping.

Angus looked up from his book. "What, boy? You have your cake. Don't you want it?"

"It's all broken. I can't eat broken cake. I want another piece. You've got to go back and get me another one." His face was scrunched up in anger, and he thrust the battered confection Angus' direction.

"Come, boy, you have your cake. There's no more to be had."

"Your fault." The boy's face contorted with emotion, as he threw his accusation out. "You ruined it."

"It's alright, boy, you can still eat it. Get a spoon, and I'll make you a cup of tea to drink with it." Angus closed his book to set it aside, when the boy thrust his

43

arm forward unexpectedly.

Slam!

Down came the boy's hand onto his book, as Angus started to rise from his chair. The book fell on the floor with a thump, the cover splayed wide, and the pages crumpled underneath. Angus and the boy stared at it, and Angus turned his arm to look at the red mark on his wrist where his hand had hit the corner of the table.

"Calm down, Lucas. I'll fix your tea."

Angus rose, picked up the kettle and started toward the door to get water from the outside keg, when a projectile sailed by his face and shattered on the floor. He turned to see the boy with a defiant expression on his face. The glitter of tiny particles of glass among the liquid on the floor revealed the whisky bottle the boy had lobbed across the space, and to protect Lucas from the slivers, he reached for an old brush used to curry the mules, the kettle still in his hand. The smell of the liquid permeated the room, and he went pale with the nauseous aroma. He laid the kettle on the table and saw the damaged cake in its brown wrapper lying there. He bent to his knees and started scooping up the pieces of glass onto a paper.

"You're not my father," the boy screamed at him.

"No, I'm not." Angus sat back on his feet and looked at the child.

"You don't want me. And, I don't want you." Lucas' face was brilliant red, and his hands were balled up in fists. He ran from the room only to return swiftly

44

as a soldier passed the open doorway. The man paused, a puzzled look on his face to see Angus on his knees in the middle of a stained floor that smelled like a saloon. Angus quickly rose and closed the door.

The boy sat on the floor near the fireplace, huddled in a mess of fright, anger and loneliness. Angus finished cleaning the floor and tossed the cake and paper into the fireplace. He picked up his book and saw that it was splattered with liquor. He threw it into the fireplace and watched it burn.

*****

The rumors that the Dragoons would soon be going to Santa Fe increased, and finally it became official. A notice was tacked on the board outside the commanding officer's building, and each man read the news with awe and wonder – or with dread and despair. Angus Meldrick read the notice with relief; for his name was listed as lead freight driver, with Claymore as his assistant. It really didn't mean anything, to be first, because they would each have their own duties. The quartermaster's assistant would be the overall officer in charge of the Army wagons, with each freight driver reporting directly to him. The bonus in the positioning was the extra pay and guaranteed provisions for himself and the boy.

He had to make the decision whether to take the boy with him, but no one in the town seemed interested in the lad. Sheriff Terrill inquired of the preacher, and the good man said he couldn't afford the added expense, since he had two boys of his own. He suggested sending the child to an orphanage in New Orleans, but Angus disagreed with that idea. Mamie McDougald volunteered to keep Lucas for a few nights, but not for the months on end that Angus would be gone to Santa Fe. And, what if he didn't return? She shuttered at the thought. He discussed the problem with the major and was granted permission to take the boy, as long as he understood he was responsible for him during the long trip.

His wagon would carry the bulk of the supplies: food stuffs, weapons and ammunition, the officers' luggage, tents, and adjutant's small field table. Claymore would follow, driving the wagon with the crates of hard bread, bacon, flour, salt, coffee, beans, peas, Indian corn, sugar, molasses, rice, hominy, yeast powder, soap and lanterns.

The cooks and bakers would have their own wagon, driven by Amos Alterson, carrying the stoves and ovens, utensils and more food. Big Smalley, the smithy, would be next with his temporary forge, billows and tools. Thomas Hawthorne, just twenty-three years old, would bring up the rear with the wagon hauling hay and grain for the animals. He would carry the medicine, extra blankets, uniforms and other clothing essentials, and miscellaneous equipment. The hay wagon was built with a wide, flat bed so as to be used for an ambulance wagon if needed. As the hay and grain disappeared, the floor space was left empty for carrying the sick or wounded; the emptied wooden boxes would be used for firewood.

At Independence, Missouri, they would join the main party of the Mexican merchant caravan and settlers bound for Santa Fe. It was there, a little over a month into his caring for the boy, that he had his second catastrophic event with the child.

Lucas simply ran away.

Angus had been lucky to rent a single room in Wood Noland's Hotel in Independence for three days. The boy was given an extra cot, and Angus made himself comfortable in the bed. As the dawn was breaking over the town, the click of a closing door caught Angus' attention. He raised up on one arm, looked around the dimly lit room and discovered the boy was gone. He jumped up and tugged his trousers up and over his hips, and quickly pulled on his boots without socks. He ran from the room, and before he reached the stairs, he realized he had on no shirt. He went back for his remaining clothing, and while pulling it onto his back, as he raced down the stairs, the floorboards creaked repeatedly, telling the entire establishment of his hurried escapade into the dimly lighted corridor. The night clerk jerked when Angus came at him like a harsh wind blowing from the north.

"Did you see the boy?" Angus demanded of the clerk, his arms akimbo and his shirttails flying in the air. He frantically stopped to button his shirt, his breath coming in gasps.

The clerk pointed toward the front door, and Angus

turned and ran out. He paused on the covered veranda and looked up and down the street but saw no young boy in either direction. He turned left and walked swiftly down the empty lane, looking into alleyways and behind garbage bins. He stopped at the end of the street and turned back the other way. He poked his head into the nearest saloon, but the light was dim, and only the bartender was awake so early in the day. He got no answer for his question, so he left and tried the blacksmith's shop, but the smithy hadn't seen a boy that morning of the description that Angus gave him. Instead, he received a curt reply for interrupting the man at his work.

After a restless tour of the town, Angus returned to the hotel, in the chance the boy had come back. Not finding him, he cursed having offered to take the child. Now angry, both for his wasted effort, extra expense and the lack of sleep during the night, he packed his bag and left the room. The child only had what he'd been wearing, and apparently, he'd dressed himself before sneaking out. The only things he'd left behind were the two stones from that first day in Saint Louis. Angus dropped them into his bag, paid the clerk for the night's lodging and a meal for the boy, ate a skimpy breakfast, and headed toward the encampment. The camp was a mass of humanity and animals. The mules and oxen were braying and lowing, kicking and generally being their obnoxious selves. He captured the six mules that he used for his wagon, leaving them in the care of the blacksmith and a private assigned to that duty to be shod.

They stayed two more days at Independence, waiting for another, larger group of freighters and pioneers from Missouri to join the caravan. The new band of freighters and pioneers were rumored to be two days away, so the Army delayed to escort them along the trail to Santa Fe. Ruthless men were opposed to the caravans crossing their land, and it had become a common practice over the previous fifteen years for troops of soldiers to escort the caravans to protect them from Indian raiders and Texas bandits harassing the Mexican traders bound for Chihuahua.

Angus kept out a watch for the boy, just in case he showed up with one of the other drivers, or he was found holed up in one of the supply wagons. Angus had already discovered that small boys had a mind of their own, although he'd been less successful in figuring out how they actually worked. It was nothing he had control over, and he spent his time doing the job he was paid to do.

Rumors abounded about the possible annexation of Texas, and Angus and his friends scanned the news-papers for news. Angus heard from a friendly captain that the Army escort would cease at Santa Fe, and the men return to either Jefferson Barracks or Fort Leavenworth in Kansas Territory, while the traders continued south into the interior of Mexico.

At last, a man from the saloon told him he had seen a boy of Lucas' description sitting near the river bank. He ran to the site, and there was the boy, muddy and disheveled, holding a branch with a string tied to one end. He'd attached a lump of bacon fat with a crude knot and was dipping it into the water on the chance a fish would bite. Breathing a sigh of relief, Angus dropped to the ground beside the boy. He caught Lucas off guard, and the boy jerked at the presence of the hated man. A look of pure fright was in the boy's eyes, and he tried to rise and escape, but Angus grabbed his arm and held him fast.

"Look, Lucas, if you don't want to live with me, I can understand that. But, what will you do? Where will you go?" When the boy relaxed in his grip, he released him, picked up a pebble and threw it into the water. He watched the small splash it created, and the ripples made a circle that grew wider and moved into the center of the river and disappeared. He stole a look at the boy when he didn't answer, and he pulled the two stones he'd been carrying from his shirt pocket. "You left so fast you forgot these. I thought you might want them back. Are you hungry? We could go and have a meal, while we discuss what's to be done. Would you like that?"

"I'm catching a fish." Lucas still held his branch, but now it dragged in the water. He eyed the two stones, as if taking them might be a compact he didn't want to make.

"Maybe the men in camp already caught some fish, and they'd be willing to share them with us. What do you think of that?"

"I want biscuits and gravy, and eggs, and ham. Can

I have that, Mr. Angus?"

"Certainly. Of course, it's not time for breakfast, so we may have to do with stew and hoecakes until morning time. Can you wait on your biscuits until then?" Lucas smiled, and he gently brushed the boy's hair back from his face. When the boy didn't jerk away, he patted him on the shoulder. "Ready to head back to camp?"

Lucas held out his hand for the stones, and he tucked them into a pocket. As soon as they had dined on a fabulous spread of boiled beef with vegetables and biscuits, he seemed more agreeable to staying with Angus. Amos Alterson was of the opinion that a couple days hunger resolved many a runaway's desire to be independent, especially if they were five years old. His observation brought a laugh from the cook and several of the cook's helpers.

While they were encamped, Angus explained to the boy his job as driver of the freight wagon. He went over the supplies on his wagon, who'd be using them, as well as why they would assume the first position in the line of supply wagons. He told him the names of his mules, showed him how to care for them and let the boy help attach their harnesses one morning. To help him feel a part of the wagon train, Angus bought Lucas a wide-brimmed hat to keep the sun from his delicate skin and a large scarf to tie around his neck. These extra luxuries made a hole in his savings and almost thrust him into penury, if not for his Army allotment, but he didn't regret the purchases. He bemoaned the fact that he'd used the previous wooden crates for firewood, as he had to ask the carpenter for a caulked wooden box for their small cache of personal items.

It was a strained relationship at first, but soon Lucas adjusted to the presence of the soldiers and the accompanying Mexican merchant wagons. He began to recognize many of the soldiers, as he was the lone child in the soldiers' company, and they began speaking to him as they walked or rode by. At times it was no more than an arm raised and a hallo, but other times, there were small trinkets or hand-carved toys dropped off.

At last, the caravan started out from Independence in the early part of June. The wagons and loose cattle and horses stretched for over a mile, three and four abreast, consisting of perhaps two hundred oxen, one hundred fifty mules, a large herd of saddle horses, thirty-two wagons, three carriages – of which a large, covered one carried the principal Mexican trader's wife, accompanied by a Dearborn loaded with servants – the army wagons, and trailing far behind, a flock of sheep, guarded by hounds and walking Spanish shepherds.

The civilian pioneers traveling to Santa Fe had brought along chickens, ducks, pigs and milk cows from Missouri. Men in fringed buckskin and beaver caps or town suits with high stiff collars and newly purchased felt hats rode horseback, with long guns and carbines poised for trouble; women walked several yards away to keep from choking on the dust raised by the train. It must have been a wonderful sight to behold, if seen from the ramparts of a building. If a man on a horse sat on a high ridge, he wouldn't be able to distinguish the Army wagons from the merchants, but up close they were notable by the initials U. S. burned on the canvas and wagons. It was the brand of the horses, mules and supplies of the Federal Government on the march.

Angus kept a watch over the boy who rode on the seat beside him. He regaled him with tales of his boyhood home and of the dog named Spot whom he had loved.

Angus made a bed for himself and Lucas on the first night of camping on the trail in the old tent he had found to cover the trunk. Their large tent was conical in shape with a center pole, and contained nothing but a selection of bedding, pillows for sitting and the carpetbag brought from Natchez. Inside the bag was an extra set of clothing for the boy in case he got wet or cold. It also kept his personal items, shaving soap, comb, brush, looking glass and a packet of soda for brushing his teeth. He had no table or chairs, since his wagon was filled with supplies and equipment for the Army. Their personal belongings in the wagon bed consisted of the trunk, filled with clothing and other essentials, and one wooden box in which was stored the kettle, two cups, two spoons, a few food items, coffee, sugar, tea and canned milk and a few toys for the boy: a slingshot, a bag of clay marbles and a set of ten tiny cast iron soldiers that Angus had bought in St.

Louis.

The smaller tents for the soldiers were in essence only a square of canvas spread across a long pole and held in place with cords at each of the four corners tied to metal pegs hammered in the ground. The men often slept in the open under the stars. They were snug and comfortable on clear warm nights, but in case of heavy weather or rain, they would take shelter inside the tents. The dirt floors were often packed hard or littered with stones or tree roots.

They made the first large camp at Lone Elm, about thirty-five miles from Fort Leavenworth, and circled the wagons, with the loose cattle, mules and horses inside. The grass was tall and plentiful, but there were no trees, only small bushes or shrubs. For many of the pioneers, it was the start of the deprivations that they would encounter along the trail. Those who hadn't brought extra wood for the fires were forced to collect animal dung, which smoked and gave off a pungent odor. Angus and Lucas, being part of the army contingent, ate their meals provided by the cooks and bakers.

From Lone Elm, they continued in a southwesterly pattern to the Kaw Mission where a treaty had been made in a grove of trees, which resulted in the eventual removal of the Comanches, who had demanded compensation from white settlers moving across their lands. From there, the caravan moved along the Arkansas River to Bent's Fort in Colorado Territory.

The river crossings were taken diagonally, the water streaming from the body of the wagons, and the mules pulling with all their strength, their heads erect and tails dragging in the wash of their bodies. Since Angus was in the front wagon, he kept the reins loose and let the animals do the work. He could see the Dragoons' mounts bobbing in the current. The banners and flags had been sheathed to protect the delicate cloth. His wheels spun, and he tightened his grip; the wagon tilted to one side, and he shifted his weight, telling Lucas to hang on tight. At last, the lead mules touched solid earth and rose out of the water; the swing and wheel mules followed, and the water dripped from the wagon as Angus pulled it to a stop under a cluster of cottonwoods and willows. He watched the Dragoons as their horses pranced and shook the water from their manes and tails.

He heard Claymore cursing behind him, a signal that he, too, had safely crossed. He secured the reins and helped Lucas alight from the wagon. They stood silently watching as wagon after wagon and countless horsemen and animals entered and exited the river. His heart thumped rapidly at every sign of disaster, but all crossed safely. The order was given to continue the march, and he lifted Lucas onto the seat. He mounted his own place on the driver's side and released the brake. His whip lightly flicked the rump hairs of the wheel mule, and the train was on the move again.

*****

Angus sat comfortably on the wagon seat, almost

dozing in the afternoon sunshine. The boy trudged alongside carrying a long stick, haphazardly striking it against rocks or the round road apples left by the traveling horses and mules. They were approaching Red Wolf Creek, and he expected to stop for a while, to give the mules a breather and fill the barrels with the clear, sparkling water. There was a long row of willows and shrubbery along the bed, and it would provide welcome relief from the heat, if they were allowed a time to rest under the shade. The ground was uneven, broken by deep arroyos and dry creek beds.

Suddenly, from his left flank, rode about a dozen riders, appearing as from under the ground, yelling obscenities and firing weapons at the Mexican traders' wagons behind him. He instinctively yelled to the boy as he pulled at the reins of the mules.

"Heh, boy, jump into the wagon."

The boy ran for the wheel and scampered up and into the conveyance, the stick still in his hand, as Angus brought the huge beasts to a halt, mere feet from the hospital wagon, whose driver had stopped so abruptly that the lead mule fell to his knees and screamed out in protest.

A sergeant rode by yelling for the wagons to circle, and Angus followed Claymore's wagon and the hospital wagon into a close formation that resembled a circle and stopped his team.

In the meantime, on his left side and a few yards ahead, he saw that Captain Ben Zolcroft of F Company had caused his men to dismount and were now formed in a line of defense. He could hear the boom of the weapons and saw one of the bandits go down. The smoke from the guns and the dust of the activity caused him to cough, and he took the cotton scarf from around his neck and made a mask to cover his nostrils and mouth. He told the boy to raise his cloth from his neck and do the same.

The boy was hunkered behind the seat, his eyes wide with fright, and didn't seem to hear him. Tying the reins loosely to the brake of the wagon, Angus climbed over the seat and showed the boy what to do with his neckerchief, then grabbed the musket from beneath the seat and began to search for bandits to kill; but the battle seemed to be coming along without his assistance.

Private John Floyd rode up to the wagon and demanded ammunition for his troopers; and telling the boy to stay under the seat, they opened one of the wooden boxes, and the Dragoon left at a gallop back to his companions. Angus began to sweat and grumble to himself at the danger the boy was in. Lucas came and huddled next to him, his small body warm and reassuring, and Angus gave him a hug.

Peeking over the leather of the wagon seat, Angus could see that the bandits were strung out in a line almost hidden by the brush between the formation of F Company and the creek, thus cutting off the Army's access to the water. He could make out several herdsmen holding the animals to the rear, thus protecting them from the bullets flying in a cascade of loud bangs and booms. He could see one Dragoon was injured, but not seriously, a shoulder wound, perhaps. The surgeon and his assistant ran to his aid, bending low to protect themselves from the attack. Puffs of dust rose from the ground near them as they cautiously dragged their wounded comrade to safety. Angus gave a sigh of relief and turned his eyes as he heard the bugle sound.

Captain Ross Quinten brought up his C Company from the back of the train and encircled the wagons, ready for battle. There were some light artillery guns included in his charge, and he had his men turn them to fire at the bandits. The mighty cannons roared in a thunderous explosion, and the bandits turned at this new challenge. Angus saw several mount their horses and ride away, as the cannon sounded its death knell again. At least three bodies lay on the ground.

Angus and the other Army supply wagons were now filling the space between two fronts of action: before and behind with the Mexican trader's wagons on the opposite side of the ridge, almost hidden by the scrub bushes and top of the arroyo. One lone tree stood majestically on the ridge as though in ignorance of the carnage going on around it.

"Are those the bad men?"

"Heh?" It was the first real thing the boy had said since the incursion started, and Angus diverted his attention from the battle to the small child at his side.

"The men shooting at us, are they the bad men?" The boy was clear-eyed, and his voice was even.

"They probably want our livestock and other supplies." The popping of musket fire and cannon punctuated his words, and twice they ducked behind the seat. The second time, Lucas' face was next to his, and the boy whispered his next question.

"Will we kill them first?"

"Or drive them away. I think our side will be happy if the bad men all go away and leave us alone."

"You're not a bad man anymore, are you?" Lucas' face was pressed against Angus' chest, and the boy had both his arms wrapped around the man.

Angus watched the top of the boy's head for a moment, and he wrapped him tightly with his arm. Above them, smoke and dust had begun to fill the air. He whispered, "No, I'm not the bad man, anymore."

"We're safe, right?" Lucas looked up, and his eyes were damp with tears.

"As safe as I can keep us." Angus smiled, and the boy smiled back.

One of the straps holding the gray canvas cover came loose and began to flap in the breeze, and Angus quickly scrambled to tie it again. A bullet buzzed his head like an angry bumble bee, and he yelled to the boy to cover his head with the collar of his coat. Turning back around, he saw a couple of the bandits leave their horses and lift their fallen comrades onto empty beasts, and soon the whole party rode away, a large dust cloud covering their retreat.

Sudden silence covered the field where the confrontation had ensued, and Angus lifted Lucas up and into his arms and gave him a hug. He was trembling like an aspen leaf in the wind. With his voice gruff from emotion, he told Lucas to help him with the wagon cover. They tied the cord more tightly and straightened the crates that had been shifted during the battle. He drew his canteen from under the seat, gave the boy a drink and tasted the tepid water for himself. Placing it back where it belonged, he and the boy jumped from the wagon. He ran to Claymore and asked if he was alright. The man replied that he was, and Angus moved on to the hospital wagon, the boy trailing a foot behind him.

The wounded Dragoon was being attended to by the surgeon and helped into the hospital wagon, despite his protest that he wasn't hurt badly. The wagon drivers mounted their seats, and Angus led them from the protective circle to the creek bank where he and his fellow waggoneers filled the water barrels and watered their animals. The Dragoons brought their animals to the water and lined up for their turn at the cool, fast-moving stream.

Angus soon learned, among the gossip of the men, that one of the bandits was left behind, taken prisoner by the captain of F Company, and was being interrogated, but Angus wasn't close enough to see or hear them. Various rumors were spreading among the troopers and the drivers, not all of which could be true. Sergeant Dixon rode down the line telling them that they would make camp for the night. Angus breathed a sigh of relief, and he watched as Lucas took out his bag of marbles. He watched the boy play while he built a fire and prepared the tent for the night. He checked on his mules and his wagon for damage, the boy following him like a leech, asking questions that Angus couldn't answer. The cook and his helpers soon had a meal prepared, and Angus and the boy ate a hearty supper, and lay close together during the night.

*****

Soon they left the Arkansas and civilization behind. The boy now seemed somewhat resigned to his daily travail of riding on the monotonous road. Sometimes he walked along, muttering to himself and poking at objects with his stick. Other days he dozed most of the hours in the back of the wagon and was ready to run and play at sunset, but Angus kept him under control. Occasionally, Lucas picked up interesting-looking stones, and Angus warned him against the poisonous snakes of the plains. At night, the wind howled across the prairie, the coyotes wailed and the mules brayed when forced to obey the drivers. The Dragoons sang or talked quietly near the cook's tent, or invented games to keep themselves busy. If the camp was set up early enough, they participated in ball games using a rolled-up ball of twine or raced each other across the grass, wearing nothing but their drawers. Often, a game of horseshoes would commence, and the clang of the metal discs rang out in the still, dry air.

The Army officers and civilian planners decided to

take the Cimarron Route instead of the more daunting and treacherous passage over Raton Pass, where the wagons would have traveled single file because of the craggy inclines and sheer drop-offs on the sides. The narrow, steep passage was on the right several miles away, and Angus took his fill of the sight of the towering Sangre de Cristo Mountains. They passed large boulders, crossed steep hills, and smelled the fragrance of pines, junipers, and spruce trees. The land eventually became rockier and rougher, but it was flat, dry and easier to travel, although the mules remained cantankerous and stubborn when brought from the rope corrals in the early mornings to be hitched to the wagon. Alterson, in particular, had trouble of a morning with the mules, and a few weeks past Pawnee Creek, one broke away from him, and the Dragoons rode after it and brought it back to the embarrassment of the young muleskinner.

Angus became more aware of the isolation and frustration of the boy when they were alone and told him interesting stories to amuse him. The tension between the men of the train increased with the miles. Angus met a few of the civilian merchants and brought a middle-aged couple with two children to visit, and Lucas brightened for a while. The children, two boys, ran wildly among the wagons, and Lucas with his shorter legs soon tired of the games. The woman's name was Thelma Carter, from Ohio, and the children were Rufus and Percival. The visits eventually tapered off after a day or two, and Thelma stayed among her own people.

— 4 —

One evening, as he and the boy were wandering along the bank of a stream, Angus took out his knife and cut one long, thick branch and several smaller limbs from a tree and took them back to the camp. He shaped the longer branch, found some thin cords among the contents of the wagon and made a bow. The smaller limbs he made into arrows and set up a target against a tree. He showed the boy how to string the bow and shoot the arrows. Satisfied that he had found a new way of entertaining the boy, he was surprised two days later when Captain Zolcroft of F Company walked up with a red-faced, angry little boy held in his left hand, with his right hand holding a bow and some arrows.

"This your boy, Meldrick?" The captain tried to control his voice, but he was most upset. "He shot an arrow into the Sanderson camp and almost hit Mrs. Sanderson's dog as she sat on a rock beside their tent. You keep the boy under control, you hear me, Meldrick?" He threw the bow and arrows on the ground, let go of the boy's arm and turned away. Angus blew out his cheeks as the man departed, and he turned to the boy. There was a guilty look in the child's stance, as he dug into the dirt with his shoe.

"I didn't mean no harm, Mister Angus. The dog tried to bite me. I didn't try to hit him, just make him go away." A lone tear fell from an eye and rolled down his cheek.

"That's alright, Lucas. But, I'm afraid I'll have to take the bow and arrows away from you until you're older. You understand?" He picked up the bow and arrows and climbed into the wagon to place them under the seat. He jumped down from the wheel and watched as the boy sulked under a tree. He sat beside the boy, explaining that he felt bad for Lucas, but it wasn't right to have the captain of the Dragoons angry over loose arrows flying about camp. Lucas huffed, and for a time they sat next to each other, neither saying a word, just watching the activity around them as the cook and bakers prepared the evening meal. It was a lonely bed they shared inside the tent that night, with the boy snuggled close to him for warmth.

*****

Increasingly, the landscape consisted of greasewood, chaparral, clumps of grass, barrel cactus and hard-packed earth mixed with sand. The pungent scent of creosote was strong. A plateau could be seen in the distance, revealing an unearthly beauty of purple haze and puffy white clouds. The land was flat, almost featureless, unforgiving and monotonous. It seemed as though a vast emptiness engulfed them, and the train was the only life along the rugged line of prairie sod. Reality was the wagons, the men on horseback, the mules and themselves, mired in silence and bitter regret.

Angus saw antelope galloping across the expansive lonely space. Once he chuckled at the antics of the ground rodents perched on their dirt mounds, still and silent. A couple of troopers broke ranks and raced toward them, and they quickly scampered into the holes, to the amusement of the men and the chastisement of their sergeant. Deep bison tracks were seen by the scouts, and a party of soldiers went looking for them but came back empty-handed. The buffalo wallows were dry, indicating they were long gone from the area.

A small group of Indians was seen on the distant horizon. A day later, they seemed to pop out of the grass beside the caravan, maybe eighteen in all. Angus was too far away to see them clearly, but although he wasn't an expert on Indian tribes, as they talked with the Dragoons, he determined they were either Pawnee or Ute. They stayed talking for some time. One gaunt rider caked with red and yellow paint rode his horse by the supply wagons, making threatening signs with his lance and yelling out, but he didn't attack, only turned back to his band of riders.

Angus had time to get down and stretch his legs. The wagons and carriage behind him stopped. Men and women of the civilian wagons stood around and gawked but didn't venture closer. A couple of the Indians were tall and gangly, but most were squalid and squatted on their haunches while the men talked and made signs; their horses looked rangy and half-starved, their ribs clearly showing under the edge of their blankets. He could see the shine of their oily, stringy hair, crusted with dirt. The few women remained on horseback behind and slightly to the left. He could see one woman with a dangling cradleboard on her back and a child of maybe a year old sitting in front of her. A couple of youngsters, maybe eight or ten years of age, sat on their horses as still as statues.

Captain Zolcroft and one of the sergeants brought the two leaders to Angus' supply wagon and dug around in the back for some meat and a few old blankets. Up close, Angus could see the scalps hanging from their lances, and he shuddered. He was close enough to tell that the men had coarse, heavy, pockmarked features. Lucas poked his head from the open canvas but quickly ducked back in when one of the Indians glanced his way. A couple of old steers were driven from the herd. One of the Indians rode up to drive the cows. They slowly moved off toward the way they had come, and Angus sighed with relief. As if by magic, they disappeared as silently as they had appeared. A double guard was detailed for the next few days, but the tribesmen weren't seen again.

Slowly, the days turned to weeks, and Angus was fortunate to drive ahead of the other wagons, his eyes scouting for trouble. When he was in camp, he tried his best to entertain the boy, telling him stories of the past, and teaching him how to recognize tracks in the dirt, or to carve letters to make words. Occasionally, he took the boy in the saddle with him as he rode around the night camp as part of his civilian duty.

Twice Angus noticed Lucas leaving the camp and strolling toward the Army fires. He brought him back to camp, explaining that the troopers didn't have time to entertain civilians. Then he had to explain the difference between Army men and the supply drivers who followed them on their excursions. He noticed in particular one man, Lieutenant Jacob Selwig, who seemed impressed by the boy's bold adventures. He was tall and slender, and clean shaven as required by his rank, but Angus was nervous of his influence. He cautioned Lucas about the soldier, that while the man may seem friendly, he had soldiering to do and couldn't spend time with a boy.

On one occasion, while he was driving the wagon, the boy wandered off, and Angus found him with the lieutenant. He had to punish the boy for his disobedience, and the lad argued with him. Afterward, Angus lay in the gloomy shadows unable to sleep, listening to the night sounds of the camp until he thought it must be close to daybreak. He rose and dressed in his stained trousers and boots and sat as still as death near his fire pit outside the tent, cold and withdrawn until the cook and his helpers began to stir. He quickly went into the tent to finish dressing and angrily trudged to his mules.

At last, they arrived at Bent's Fort. He took the boy to the store and bought him a new pair of trousers. He splurged on a cake of soap and a toy hoop for the boy to roll along the ground as he walked. It took the last of his script, and he had only a few coins left in his pocket. He refused to become entangled in debt, and it was a few weeks before payday, if they got paid at all.

They left Bent's Fort on a hot, cloudless day and started on their journey southwest. Lucas kept under the shade as much as possible, but still his forehead and the top of his hands became sunburned. Angus smeared them with axle grease, but they became caked with mud, and he had to wash it off. The boy stayed mostly in the wagon, under the canopy. He ignored the hoop that Angus had bought for him. Angus' lips grew chapped and his skin dry and his face haggard. Their hair was coated with dust, and the blowing sand made their eyes feel gritty and stung like tiny needles on exposed skin. The animals were in worse shape; and everyone suffered from the brackish, dirty water. On and on they traveled until at last, a scout yelled that Taos Pueblo was seen a few miles away.

The higher altitude and cooler air was a welcome respite for all: civilians and military men alike. The large Pueblo made up the major part of the town, consisting of adobe houses and surrounded by short, stubby vegetation. A few chickens pecked the ground inside vertical pole fences. Inside the plaza were beaver trappers, Spanish settlers and Indians wandering about. A high peak stretched skyward in the distance. The troops and merchant wagons turned south and rolled on toward Santa Fe.

Two days before arriving at the outskirts of Santa Fe, Lucas was sitting beside Angus on the wagon seat.

"Mister Angus, can I get down and walk?" The boy was watching the troopers as they rode by, their backs stiff and their banners hanging limply in the calm air. The animals looked gaunt and tired.

"No, stay in the back where it's cooler, boy." A Dragoon pulled away from the riders in formation ahead of them and rode almost out of sight.

Angus caught a glimpse of the man's blue coat and brown horse standing beside the trail. He recognized the lieutenant by his uniform and blond, almost yellow hair, as he walked in the heat of the mid-day sun. Angus kept a tight control on the reins of the mules, only cursing under his breath at his foolishness. The boy popped his head up from the back of the wagon, and Angus turned for a moment to speak to him. The boy had a slingshot in his hand.

"Can I get down, now? I can shoot some birds for dinner." He bragged with his eyes bright and glowing with unshed tears.

"No, son, you had best remain inside the wagon where it's safe."

The boy withdrew back into the space behind the seat, where a comfortable place had been made for him among the crates. They rode on for some time, the wagon jostling against the uneven ground, and rocking where wagon ruts from previous caravans had formed trenches in the soil. Lucas' haven in the wagon was snug and secure, with blankets and pillows, his own private tent in which to play and sleep. He put the slingshot away and took out his toy soldiers from the small wooden box in which they were stored.

"Mister Angus, which one is the captain?" He popped through the canvas again with a toy soldier in a red tunic and tiny carbine in the folds of the metal cloth. "I want to play with him, but I don't know who he is."

It was at that moment that Angus heard a gunshot and saw several Dragoons ride swiftly towards the place where he had last seen the lieutenant. There was a great shout, and he tried to turn his mules to escape the congestion but was hemmed in by a sudden convergence of horses and men on foot. A rider galloped toward the rear of the column of wagons. There were about fifteen minutes of confusion before Paulson, a sergeant, came to tell him that the lieutenant had been snake bitten. Angus stopped the team, set the brake on the wagon, jumped down and yelled urgently for Lucas to remain with the soldier.

He ran toward the center of the circle of men, about ten minutes, and they made way for him when they recognized his anxiety. They all stood in a circle as if

70

consumed by shock. He found Lieutenant Selwig on the ground, writhing in pain, froth issuing from his mouth and his face pale and clammy. The dead snake had been tossed a few feet away. He glanced at it and cringed.

"I've sent someone for the surgeon; best let him through when he comes. I hope he arrives soon." It was Lieutenant Packard who spoke, his blue eyes vibrant in his pale, freckle-covered face. He was an officer who spoke to Angus regularly and who seemed to be of a general good nature. It was likely to be an hour or more, as they well knew. The surgeon had to be located, first, then make his way to the scene of the injury. Packard's hat was missing from his head, and his hair was thick and coated with dust. He stood with a gun still in his hand. He seemed to become conscious of it and put it back in the holster and fastened the flap. His sword hung loosely at his side.

"What happened? You were here; what happened?" Angus' words came out angrily, barely short of a verbal lashing. The lieutenant's face whitened with shock and fear. Angus frowned, and Selwig's shaking began again. His face turned pale as Lieutenant Selwig continued muttering and tossing from side to side. "I'm trying to understand how this could happen so quickly. I saw the lieutenant draw away from his men and stand along the trail just minutes before. He was in fine form."

"It was a rattler, Angus. He suddenly sprang from the rocks, and before I was aware, he struck his ankle.

I shot him, but I couldn't stop the poison from entering his body. He fell to the ground and lay so still." Packard hung his head, and Angus let it go.

"You go get some water, sir. There's nothing to be done now." Angus knelt at the injured man's side, as some of the other men began to drift away. Angus sent for a damp cloth to soothe the man's forehead until the surgeon made his presence known. When it arrived, he folded it into a long rectangle, laid it over the man's forehead, and held it with his hand so that it didn't get knocked off as the man writhed from side to side.

The wait was interminable, with the sun beating down, and the man growing more and more agitated. A few men still stood around, although the event had lost much of its interest for the most experienced of the Army men. Death by snake bite was not uncommon in the Southwest, and this man's demise wasn't likely to be the last.

Angus stood at the surgeon's arrival and moved aside. Rory McCutchen was a gaunt figure, with wide shoulders and a peppery mustache. His face showed the years he'd spent in the Army, and his eyes narrowed at the scene before him. McCutchen threw his old worn black satchel on the ground and opened it. Inside glistened shiny instruments and bottles and tins of salve. The doctor took a knife and split the lieutenant's boot leather, tossed the boot remnants aside and rolled his trouser leg. The ankle was black and purple and swollen.

"Doc? What are his chances? I mean, that's pretty

serious, a snake bite out here on the trail." Angus looked around to see the men's interest returning with the arrival of the surgeon, and a crowd of onlookers had started to gather once more. Some looked concerned, but more seemed to find the event as a welcome break from the tedium of the campaign.

"I don't know, Angus." McCutchen shook his head. "I'm sorry I couldn't get here sooner. I was treating a minor case of gout for one of the settlers, and I thought the shouting was a game to pass the time. How long's it been since the bite?" He gave the injured man a liquid medicine with water, but the medicine mixed with saliva erupted in a convulsive surge and slid down the side of Selwig's cheek. There was no way of knowing if the antidote reached his insides.

"Two and a half, maybe three hours by now."

"Then we'll know soon. He'll either die or begin to recover. Move back, Angus, and give me room," the surgeon grumbled. But the freighter didn't budge. The lieutenant's face became distorted, and he stiffened. The doctor took out his stethoscope and listened to his heart. He lifted one eyelid and shook his head.

Angus blanched. The crush of onlookers became an unwelcome wall, and the hot sun beat unmercifully on his back. Within a few minutes, Selwig's eyes rolled inward, and he was gone.

Angus stepped away. His face was flushed as he was jostled by the crowd of men as he stepped back. The surgeon must have had his men waiting nearby, for they wrapped the fallen officer in a blanket and lifted him onto the hospital wagon. The driver, Zeke Alcott, leaped on the wagon seat and turned it toward the tail of the army troops. The men began to drift away. The doctor remained behind.

"The boy. I have to go to the boy," Angus muttered. He shook his hands, one at each side, and brushed them along his shirt, leaving damp stains.

The doctor stepped forward, his black bag in hand, and his salt-and-pepper mustache dulled by a coating of dust. "It couldn't be helped, Angus. These southwestern rattlers are deadly."

"I need to get to the boy. He'll have to be told. He liked the lieutenant."

"That's the Griswold boy, right? Adam was a good man. It's a shame what happened to him. You're doing the boy a great favor, providing for the youngster." McCutchen placed a hand on Angus' shoulder and clapped it once before releasing it.

"Thanks, Doc."

Angus walked to his wagon, relieved the kind sergeant of his duty and told the boy the sad news. Lucas had his toy soldiers out, and he continued to play as Angus spoke with him. Angus couldn't wait to see if the boy would become upset, as he had to regain his place in the formation. There was no time available to commiserate with the child until nightfall.

The wagons continued to roll until sunset when the colonel called a halt for the night. Immediately upon settling the wagon and unhitching the mules, Angus took the boy's hand and walked toward the rear of the camp, away from the other men, trying to protect the boy from the smell of death. Orders were given for a grave to be dug beside the trail, and the army chaplain sat with the blanket-wrapped body until the service began. A large crowd of civilians, merchants and farmers, soldiers and officers stood around the grave while the chaplain read from the Bible and said a prayer. One of the privates started singing, and the audience joined in. The sound echoed through the hills and night air. The hole was filled in, and everyone began to disperse for their campfires and wagons.

The cooks and bakers had continued with the preparations for the nighttime meal while the ceremony was going on, and Angus took the boy to their usual place in line behind the soldiers with the other drivers and civilian support group. Life in the familiar merchant caravan with its military escort went on as usual, with conversation among the men, ribald jokes and the occasional complaints about the quality of the food. Angus and Lucas waited their turn in line and squatted beside the wagon with their plates. Angus ate a small portion of his meal before he set the rest aside. The boy consumed everything on his plate except for several carrots, which he pushed off to one side. When Lucas asked him if he wasn't hungry, Angus held up a hand to show that it was shaking with nervous energy. He told him he still felt a bit dizzy after the events of the afternoon, and he didn't think he could hold down a complete meal. The boy nodded and pulled the two stones from the inside of one pocket and began to toss them in the air and catch them. When he missed, he laughed, brushed the dirt off, and tried again.

Angus dug a hole in the soil, scraped the remains of their food inside, and covered it before returning the soiled plates and utensils to the cook's wagon. He saw that the boy was washed and bedded, and he sat alone under the stars, a lonely, troubled man. The strum of a guitar filled the night air, soon joined by the whine of a fiddle, and Angus finally smiled. Everything was normal at the camp. The familiar sounds enfolded him; his companions laughed or played poker; and his duties were done for the night.

— 5 —

Arriving in the valley that held the usually sleepy Mexican adobe town of Santa Fe, the sound of fireworks and music punctuated the air in the distance. Angus had been in Santa Fe before, about five years previously with an Army expedition out of Fort Leavenworth. He was somewhat familiar with the streets and buildings of the town. He told stories to Lucas about his time there to gauge what the boy might think about it, telling him they might find a small house, or a hotel room, while they were there. The sound of distant bells coming from the church steeple broke though the heat and dust of the day, and both Angus and Lucas laughed at the same time, smiling at the clear and beautiful sounds coming across the barren landscape.

Here the civilians and the Army separated and made two camps along the banks of the river that flowed through the city. The banks next to the water were muddy, but grass was abundant, and stretches of the shore were littered with willows. They created pockets of shade along the water, making the campsites very appealing. Angus pulled his wagon next to Claymore, the other supply driver, the cooks and the hospital wagon. They made a circle, unhitched the teams and tied them securely in a rope corral inside the circle. Two of the privates were assigned the task of guarding them. Scrounging in the wagon, Angus pulled out his canvas tent, and climbing awkwardly over the side, threw it onto the ground and went back for the pole and stakes.

"Lucas, do you remember where we keep the hammer?" His head was in the wagon, and he continued to probe for the tool.

The boy looked at the wagon with a puzzled frown, then his face brightened, and he clambered up the wheel and into the wagon. Angus caught sight of him and withdrew a short distance to watch the boy. Lucas soon appeared with the hammer in his hand, and he jumped from the wagon, landing on his backside in the dirt. Angus put his hands on the child's shoulders, pulled him to his feet and complimented him on his success.

Together, they spread the tent fabric and began assembling their temporary home. As Angus was driving the last stake in the ground, he glanced up, with hammer in hand, to see Captain Nelson, the assistant quartermaster, approaching, with two troopers trailing behind him, Garrett and Patterson. He gave him a greeting and grinned at the two troopers, who stood politely at attention.

Nelson gazed at the boy, who had squatted in the dirt and was playing with his marbles. One of the marbles escaped, and the captain picked it up and handed it to the boy.

"Say, Meldrick, we've come for the colonel's gear, and some extra weapons and ammunition." Nelson stood with his hands behind his back, looking over the scene, his eyes resting on the canvas-covered wagon for a moment, before reaching into a flattened, tailored pocket to withdraw a cigarillo and a phosphorus friction match. He struck it, creating a flash and a blaze of flame and lighting his smoke. He drew in two quick puffs and tossed the used match to the ground and twisted one foot atop it.

"Certainly, sir," Angus replied, resting the hammer on the ground at his side, and he stood.

"We've made good time, heh, Meldrick? If you're of a mind, I'll have my men retrieve the gear we need. I can see you're busy with your tent and the boy."

"We're about finished, here. I'm glad to help."

Garrett and Patterson were already at the wagon taking out the supplies they had come for and putting them on the ground. Angus climbed in to show them the specific crates for those items they hadn't yet located. He handed the requested items one at a time to

Garrett who handed them to Patterson who laid each one on the ground.

When the requisition didn't go as quickly as he expected, Nelson yelled, "Claymore? I need you over here to help sort these items from the lead wagon. Claymore?"

Claymore came running, and with his help, they soon had the captain's supplies sorted out. They needed a small cart to transport them, and Nelson sent one of his men to locate one. In the interim, Nelson walked to stand beside Angus and cleared his throat before speaking.

"I say, Meldrick, you've been here before; tell me the address of a good restaurant." He smirked and winked. "One with fine company afterwards, for female companionship. You understand my meaning. About the boy, I knew his father, you know, good man, Adam Griswold. Has the boy any memory of the man?"

"Not that I've heard him say. Sir, I believe your supplies are ready." Angus nodded to where the men had finished with the collection of supplies and begun to move towards the front of the column, carrying the boxes and crates, with the larger items on the wheeled cart.

"That's all, then." Nelson ended the conversation with his cursory remark and, exhaling a stream of white smoke from his cigarillo, he followed his men.

While the boy watched in wonder, Angus dug a small pit, walked to the river bank and gathered an armful of small logs and branches for his fire. There were plentiful loose branches under the willows, as though no one had ever collected branches from this section of the river. Angus filled Lucas's arms with a similar selection, although branches in his size, careful not to overwhelm him with the weight. He dumped them on the ground near the pit, and taking the boy's hand in his large callused one, they returned for more. They tried to be careful of their boots and trousers, but the best branches were almost on the shore, and the ground was muddy. Holding the branches on the way back to camp also created a mess, as dirt and woody material constantly scraped from the branches onto their clothing. Angus could see the head cook had set up his tables, stoves and ovens nearby. He caught a glimpse of the surgeon giving orders to some underlings to set up the hospital tent. It was a familiar sight; he had witnessed it a hundred times or more in his career with the soldiers. It was different tonight, somehow, for he had a small boy to care for.

He found an old newspaper, took out his pen knife, made some shavings from one of the branches and built a small fire. He was careful in its construction so it wouldn't smoke too much, piling the wood into a conical shape, with the shavings in a small pile underneath, and the sticks growing ever larger the farther from the center. The ends of the shavings curled ferociously, as if alive, and they danced with the slightest movement of Angus' or Lucas' hands. Lucas giggled and said they were having a party.

Angus pulled out his treasured flint, and he struck it several times with his knife before he was successful in getting the spark to land just where he wanted it. When the spark leaped into the shavings, a tiny speck of hot light, it continued to burn. Angus blew on it gently, causing it to glow brighter, until he saw a puff of flame and a thin stream of white smoke. Angus soon had a nice blaze going, and he sat and held his hands to the flame. Lucas copied his every move. He laughed.

"Well, son, we're parked here for a while. Are you hungry? I'll get you some beef jerky to tide you over until the cook gets our supper ready. You keep an eye out for him. See that man with the white apron over there? That's him. We'll soon have a full stomach, you'll see." He walked to the wagon, climbed in over the wheel and rummaged in his pack until he found some jerky wrapped in paper he had begged from the cook that morning. The boy needed his appetite satiated continually. He pulled the kettle and the cups from a crate of such items. They came in handy when there was a long wait for their meal. He climbed down, careful not to drop the utensils and the paper-covered meat.

"You stay here, boy, and don't wander off. I'm going to get some water for coffee." He admonished the lad and kept his eyes on him until he dipped the kettle into the fast-moving water; he rose and came back to the fire, the water splashing onto his boots. He returned to the wagon, brought a tin of coffee to the fire and spooned a bit into the kettle. While it was heating, he took a piece of jerky from the cloth, broke off a small chunk and handed it to Lucas.

"It looks to be a fine day tomorrow. Maybe if we can, we'll drift into the town and see what the noise is about. Sounds like fiesta time. You'll like that. I wonder if it's one of their saint's days. Want another piece?" It was a habit the man had gotten into, talking to the boy. The boy nodded his head, took the morsel from Angus' fingers and started eating. The boy held out his hand again. "No. That's enough for now. If you fill your belly, you won't need any taters and biscuits." He put the remaining jerky back in the paper and set it aside.

The coffee started perking, and the aroma filled his nostrils with anticipation.

"I'll get out the tablet and a pencil in a bit, and we'll practice your letters again. Pick up a stick and see if you can write your name in the dirt." As he was drinking his liquid refreshment, he guided the lad through his name and the name of his father, careful to keep the bitterness and sadness from his tone. "Can you remember my name? What do the men call me?"

Lucas squeezed his eyes tight, and said, "Angus." He put a long drawl in it, and Angus laughed.

"That's right; my name is Angus. Can you make an A?" For the next few minutes, he helped the boy learn to write Angus in the soil. He finished his coffee, took the boy to the river bank and brought back a bucket of water for their nightly ritual of washing before their meal. It was pleasant beside the river. The higher altitude and the on-coming night air began to cool the rays of the sun, foretelling the nights that sometimes grew cold in the mountains.

The smells from the cook's tent grew stronger and lingered. Angus took a long look at the axles of his wagon and pulled out a can of grease, talking all the while to the boy, who sat with his tablet and pencil, making squiggles on the paper, his tongue caught between his lips. Sometimes, he looked at Angus, and sometimes, he cast his gaze toward the man in the white apron.

A private appeared, heading their way.

"Hey, boy," the young man said. "I see you got a good place here close to the camp kitchen. I should be so lucky. What's your name?"

"Lucas," he piped up, with a smile.

"Good for you, Lucas. I brought a message for Mr. Angus. Is it okay if I give it to him?" The man smiled and gave him a wink.

"Of course. What's in it?"

"They don't tell me those things." He grinned and held out a folded paper to Angus. "Sir, for you. I hope it's good news." He gave the two of them a nod before heading back from whence he had come.

Angus frowned as he unfolded the missive and let his eyes rove over the precisely inked script. It was from the colonel. It said to report to him at precisely nine o'clock the next morning at his tent headquarters. He pulled his hat from his head and wiped his forehead. He groaned when he saw the boy was watching him closely. He smiled as though nothing was wrong, threw the paper in the fire and watched it blaze up and shrivel in the flames.

— 6 —

During the night, Angus was awakened by a soft,
gentle rain falling on the tent roof. The night was dark
and there was no wind, so he checked to see if the boy
was covered, then pulled the blankets over his own
shoulders, and drifted back to sleep.

Leading the boy by the hand, he obeyed the sum-
mons from the colonel the next morning, careful to
keep to the wooden planks that had been laid across the
muddy trenches that had begun to stretch unwelcome
fingers across the encampment. He left the boy with
the aide while he went in the tent to talk. He stood at
attention until the man had finished writing something
on a long piece of paper. He glanced quickly around,
but Packard wasn't there.

"Angus, please sit down."

He sat and blinked at the glare of the sun filtering

through the canvas of the tent. A few insects had infiltrated the tent during the night and clung to the cloth, either in life or death. He brought his attention back to the colonel.

"I'll need some information about the boy for the records. Get to it as soon as you can while we're in camp. The adjutant's in town, and he'll be posting some dispatches soon. Then we'll have the matter behind us. I didn't approve of bringing the boy on this excursion, but everything seems to have worked well. Do you feel the same?" Angus nodded, and the colonel continued. "Well, enough about that. I went into town last night to introduce myself and give my credentials to the local authorities. Captain Nelson will be seeing about accommodations for me in town while we're replenishing our supplies and waiting for the return trip. I understand there are a few merchants wanting an escort back to Missouri. During dinner, I spoke to the alcalde about your situation. He said there's a middle-aged American couple, a Polish merchant who trades with the Spanish and French in Chihuahua. They're on the return trip to the States; he became ill, and their trip was delayed; but now she's expressed a desire to return to their home in the East. He said she might be willing to help you with the boy, if you need her. Her name's Elmira Pulaski; has a grown daughter somewhere in Missouri, I think he said." The colonel looked sharply at Angus, whose neck grew red underneath his shirt collar.

"But, sir, I can't afford to hire a nursemaid for the

boy. I only have my salary with the Army, you know." Angus twisted his hat in agitation.

"What, man? I can see you don't approve, and it's not just the cost. Spit it out."

"I'm just getting to know the boy. I don't like the thought of a woman interfering with his care."

"You can't afford not to have her, man. You have your duties with the supply wagon and the mules; you can't spend all your time with the lad; he needs someone to nurture and teach him his manners and such things. How old is he?" The colonel reached over his table and found a tin of cigars, and taking out one and a match from his pocket, lit it and took a long draw.

"Just past six, sir. Had his birthday on the trail from Missouri. He's learned how to spell and write his name and count to ten. He's a smart boy."

"Is he? Well, that's fine. What had you planned to do with him when this trip is over?" He took another puff and looked out the wide entrance gap at some soldiers strolling by.

"I hadn't thought that far ahead, sir." Angus followed the colonel's eyes, saw a woman stop before the tent and heard a murmur of voices at the entrance. The colonel seemed to be listening to the conversation, but the words weren't plain enough to be easily made out.

"Mrs. Pulaski has her own income; you won't have to pay her to care for your boy. The Army will advance you some funds to help pay for the trip." He put out his cigar in a crockery dish on his table and stood up. He walked to the door before Angus could react and shouted at his aide.

"Corporal! Send the lady in." He stepped back and to the side and waited, with his back to Angus.

"Mrs. Pulaski, sir," the corporal announced in a pretentious voice before he withdrew. In walked a heavy, gray-haired woman dressed all in black from her heels to the small felt hat on her head.

Elmira Pulaski looked around the canvas room, and her eyes found the man in the faded blue plaid shirt and brown corduroy trousers. Angus jumped from his seat to stand beside his chair, and at almost the same time, the colonel turned to face them both.

"You sent for me, Colonel?" Elmira's voice was soft and calm.

"Yes, Mrs. Pulaski. If you'll have a seat, please."

The colonel crossed the room and guided her to a seat next to the one that had been previously occupied by Angus, the freight driver, who stared at her in consternation. She sat down gracefully and folded her hands in her lap.

"Angus, if you please." The colonel indicated Angus' chair. Angus gulped, swallowed the saliva in his mouth, and sat back down. "Mrs. Pulaski, I'm pleased to meet you. This is Angus Meldrick, one of our contracted supply drivers. Officially, he works for the Army but isn't with the military; he drives the supply wagon along with the cooks and the bakers and the hospital wagons. He works specifically under the jurisdiction of the assistant quartermaster and sometimes scouts for us when we need an extra hand. He has a small boy left bereft of a mother's love and guidance. Now, you've been telling the alcalde for months that you and Tom want to get back East to your daughter and grandchildren. We discussed the matter last night while I was at the alcalde's dinner that Meldrick might be of assistance to you and your husband. Of course, if that's agreeable to both." The colonel walked behind his table and sat down, leaving a very surprised woman and an equally shocked man gazing at him with dismay. He started shuffling his papers and picked up a book and laid it back down.

The moment grew tense with silence. The questions hung in the air. Elmira was obviously a genteel lady, and beyond the childbearing years, but was she healthy and strong enough to care for a rambunctious young child? As for Angus, he was rudely dressed and looked to be a rough character. Her glance said he was little better than a soiled spot on a rug in her eyes.

"Angus?" The colonel cleared his throat suggestively. "Now's your time to speak."

"Uh, ma'am, I don't have much in luxuries, nothing but my wagon," he paused and scratched his head, "and that ain't mine, belongs to the Army, and we eat with the soldiers. The boy's usually quiet and don't cause too much trouble. I'm teaching him his letters and numbers. As the colonel said, I have my duties and can't be with the lad all the time. You'd be most welcome to join us on the trail back to Missouri, if you'd like to come along. You'd have to ride on the wagon seat with me, of course." It was a long speech for Angus, and he drew a deep breath. Beads of sweat accumulated across his forehead.

"It's your chance, Mrs. Pulaski, to get back to civilization. What with the rumors of war on the horizon, and the politicians in Mexico City, I don't see when you might have a better chance. I'll be with the troops, and we'll give you the best protection we can, but until the railroads begin building this far, there's not much hope of transportation until next year, maybe." The colonel looked thoughtful.

"I'll have to talk it over with my husband, Colonel, and get to know the boy. How long before you start back to the States?" She fidgeted with the handbag in her lap.

"I figure it'll be a week or ten days. There's a rancher outside of town, you might know him, Johnson Emery? I hope to buy some cattle and horses from him; and I have to wait for the quartermaster to purchase his supplies, and the doctor his pills and salves." He stood up as if in dismissal. "I'll call on you tomorrow, if I may, and get some privates to help you pack if you decide to go with us."

Elmira Pulaski rose gracefully, shook the hand of the colonel and turned to Angus, who had stood politely when she did. "Mr. Meldrick, if you are free, would you escort me to your wagon so I may get acquainted with your son? That's him, outside the tent?"

Angus had no choice; he nodded in answer to her question and took the lady's arm. He ushered her from the tent, after picking up his hat, placing it on his head and saying a quick, gruff goodbye to the colonel. The whiff of a flowery perfume engulfed him as they walked. He called to Lucas, who scampered from where he'd been using his slingshot to fire rocks at the birds soaring through the thermals in the sky. The corporal gave Angus a guilty look; and Angus slipped a coin into his hand. It wasn't proper protocol, but Angus had found that the soldiers appreciated the gesture.

Mrs. Pulaski had waited patiently during the scene but now spoke up for his attention. "How old are you, Mr. Meldrick, and how long have you worked for the Army?" She stepped around a knothole in the wooden plank, and Angus was forced to shift his steps to match hers; he motioned toward the left to guide her the correct direction, and they left the officers' tents behind and walked toward the animal corrals. Lucas skipped ahead of them. The campfires of the civilian merchant wagons winked and danced in the distance, still parked outside the city. They would soon pack up and turn south to Chihuahua.

"Mr. Meldrick?"

He started at the sound of his name. "Uh, I'm thirty-two, ma'am, and I've been with the army since I was eighteen. The major at Jefferson Barracks wanted me to sign up with the military, but they're too restrictive for me; I like a little freedom, and I like working with mules. It's no hardship to drive a wagon; although it sometimes grows dangerous when the

Indians get aroused or the bandits try to steal the horses. Begging your pardon, ma'am, I shouldn't talk of such things before a lady."

"Why not? I came on a freight caravan with my husband when I was young. I'm familiar with the night crawlers and cooking over a campfire." She sighed and remained silent for a while. They were near the parked wagons when she spoke again. "When our children were small, I was left behind, but when the girls were married, I climbed aboard the wagon seat again and went to Chihuahua with my husband, Tom. We've been away for two years."

The conversation fell away for a while. Eventually, Mrs. Pulaski broached a subject that must have been on her mind since meeting Angus in the colonel's office.

"I noticed you have an old injury. May I inquire as to how you received it?" She didn't look at him but studied those walking past them with an air of nonchalance.

"I was a boy, and Indians attacked my home in Kentucky. They killed my father."

"How horrible!" Mrs. Pulaski paused and looked at him for a moment before continuing. "That doesn't explain your injury, however."

Angus cleared his throat. "The savages grabbed me and tried to scalp me. My mother escaped to the nearby Army post and raised the alarm. She was of a weak constitution, and the exertion and an injury from an arrow were too much for her. When the men found me,

I was barely alive. I lived in the Army barracks until I was seventeen, when I decided Army life wasn't for me, not as an enlisted man, anyway."

"Well, thank you, Mr. Meldrick. That was brave of you to share that. I think we'll not mention it in front of the boy."

The sun was bright on the horizon, and streaks of pink, scarlet, and gold began to color the western sky. They arrived at his wagon, and Angus could smell the scent of food cooking a few yards away where the cooks had started supper. He caught the aroma of spices and coffee, and his stomach growled.

"Here we are, ma'am. Lucas, where are you, boy? Damn, where'd he go?" His ears turned red, and he coughed. "Sorry, ma'am, forgot you were here."

"Oh, don't give it a thought; I'm accustomed to the language of men on the road."

He looked around, but the boy wasn't there. Just when he was beginning to panic, he saw him walking from the cook's tent with one of the soldiers. He looked at the woman to get her reaction to the boy's mischievous misbehavior. She smiled, and he smiled, too. The boy had his hand full of cake and had obviously eaten part of it, as there were crumbs on his mouth.

He ran to Angus, leaving a protective Private Zellers a few steps behind.

"Mister Angus, look!" He skidded to a halt when he saw the woman.

"Hello, Lucas. You must be very hungry. Private, how do you do?" Mrs. Pulaski stepped forward and

94

shook hands with the silent soldier. Lucas came cautiously closer and then hid behind his adopted father's legs, holding tightly to his food.

"Thank you, Private Zellers, I appreciate your help. Do I smell food cooking? Go on about your duties; it'll be supper soon, and I'm sure you're hungry." The private took off at a run toward his camp. "I'm sorry, ma'am, I don't have a chair. There's a rock I've been using for a seat, if you care to use it. Lucas, don't be shy. You might as well finish your cake, although you'll spoil your supper, if you eat now."

"I will be seated. Thank you, Mr. Meldrick." Mrs. Pulaski delicately lowered herself onto his rock, and having given up his only seat, Angus groaned.

"Mrs. Pulaski, I don't have any funds, just my army pay. I've not had a real home since I was a youth, so I don't have many things of my own. We eat with the troopers and the Dragoons, so you won't have the chore of cooking, just making sure the boy is safe and clean and dry when we're near a creek. He likes to play in the water."

Lucas grinned at that, then his little face scrunched up and his eyes grew damp. "Mister Angus, when's my aunty coming back? I couldn't find her when I woke up." He started to cry in earnest.

"Boy, come here." Angus squatted so he could be at the boy's level. He put his arm around his shoulders. "Son, I told you before. Your aunt can't come back to us. Do you remember? Your aunt brought you on the big boat to me; and she went back East. You belong with me, now."

Lucas looked up at the brilliant colors of the sunset and wiped his eyes on his sleeve. "But, why did she go away? I want her here with us."

Mrs. Pulaski sat quietly on the rock, needless of the dirt on her skirt hem. She pulled the boy into her lap. Angus rose and stood nearby, blowing out his cheeks with exasperation.

"Lucas, sweetheart," Mrs, Pulaski began, "way up there in the sky; do you see that first star of the night?" The boy looked and, even though the sun was still bright on the horizon, a star shown in the scarlet and gold of sunset. He nodded his head. "Honey, every night when it's about supper time, look up at the sky, and see if you can find that star. Pretend it's your mama looking down at you, and you'll never be lonely or afraid. Sometimes the angels get lonely, too, and they come for a human to live with them. I know you're too young to understand now, but when you're tall and strong and handsome like your papa, you will. Would you like for me to stay with you and ride with you in the wagon to Missouri? I can, you know. Your papa said I can, and we'll have lots of fun. We'll learn to read and write your name on paper; and how to sing and blow bubbles and throw a bean bag. Oh, lots of things."

The boy looked at her, and then at Angus. "You're my papa? But my papa's dead; the soldier told us."

"Mr. Meldrick?" She turned her eyes toward him, and Angus shook his head.

"It's true, ma'am, his papa and mama died, and he had no place to go when his aunt left him in Missouri, so I just kind of brought him with me." He shrugged. "With the Army's permission, of course."

"Mister Angus, can she go with us? I like her. Please, Mister Angus." The boy's eyes were as big as a wagon wheel. He pulled on Angus' hand, and the man couldn't refuse him.

"Yes, she can come with us to Missouri, but right now, we have to take her back to her home, so we can get cleaned up for supper. Mrs. Pulaski, thank you. I hope you don't regret your decision." He turned and saw there were tears in her eyes. She took a handkerchief from her pocket and wiped her cheeks dry. "Come, we'll walk you to your place."

They were silent for a while, and the boy skipped happily along beside them, sometimes looking up with an odd expression on his face. Once, when he wandered too far afield, Mrs. Pulaski snapped her fingers to get his attention, and she stopped and held out her hand until he came to her. For a time after that, she held his hand in hers, forcing him to stay at her side, until he quit pulling away. When she released him, admonishing him to remain closer, the boy narrowed his zone of play, and she smiled.

"You're good with him," Angus remarked.

"I've raised children, and I know what works with them." She glanced at him, but Angus just kept walking, watching the boy at play.

When they stopped at the front of a compact but

efficient-looking adobe structure, she held out her hand. "Thank you, Mr. Meldrick, I'll see you in the morning. Where should we meet? My house might be a nice quiet place. About eleven o'clock? Goodnight. Goodnight, Lucas." And, with a nod, she was gone, her skirts swirling about her ankles, a faint scent of flowers whiffing to his nostrils.

Angus turned and headed back to the army camp, muttering that he needed help with the boy, but he didn't want a woman to keep him in turmoil all the time. If the woman and her husband wanted to get back to her family in the East, perhaps he could find them transport, without them riding in his wagon.

"Mister Angus?"

"Yes, son?" Angus looked down at the boy and smiled.

"Is the lady my new mama?"

That stopped the man in his tracks. He looked at the boy in shock. "No, she isn't your mama. As of tomorrow, she'll be your teacher and companion. She said she would teach you how to read and write and sing, remember? Since you can't attend a proper school like most boys, you need a teacher to care for you. We'll get along fine, you'll see."

The next morning, Angus went to call formally on Mrs. Elmira Pulaski. He sent a message by one of the Mexican boys who had begun to hang around the camp, begging for money or jobs. She replied that she would receive him at eleven o'clock as agreed and asked if he and the boy would stay to partake of the noon meal.

He called promptly, his hair combed and neatly trimmed; his clothes were clean, although slightly wrinkled, and the boy wore his face scrubbed, with eyes red-rimmed from crying. The morning had not gone flawlessly. While doing his morning absolutions, Angus had warned the boy quite sternly to remain in the wagon, for there was no time to play, if they were to make it on time to see Mrs. Pulaski. Despite his warning, the child had climbed down from the wagon while Angus was getting ready in the tent and visited the cook's tent, begging for sweets. There had been nothing else for it but to punish him by taking away the tiny toy soldiers he loved to line up in a row and knock down in mock battles against opposing troops.

The door was answered by a young Mexican girl in a white blouse and bright blue skirt. She curtseyed and ushered them into an anteroom to sit and await their hostess. The house was cool and clean, and furnished in a practical style. Through a series of open doors, a small courtyard revealed a fountain and numerous flowering shrubs. It was an unexpected scene in the barren landscape of the desert. In a corner of the room, so quiet as to be unnoticed, sat a white-haired man, wearing a robe across his lap. The robe was woven in a zigzag pattern, with bright, earthy colors. His skin was parched and dry from many days in the sun, and his hair was a wild halo.

"My apologies, sir. We've come for an appointment with Mrs. Pulaski. The servant girl asked us to wait here."

"Come in. Come in, Mr. Meldrick. I'm Tom Pulaski, from Poland originally, but I've been in America for over thirty years. Mira says that you've volunteered to see that we get to Missouri. Is this your boy?" The man squinted at his two visitors.

"Yes, this is Lucas." Angus crossed to the chair and shook hands with Pulaski. "Is your chair wheeled, sir? It might be difficult to manage on my wagon, as my main job is to carry supplies for the Army. I have some room, as supplies are continually consumed, but this I'm unsure of. Missouri is a very long way from Santa Fe."

The man laughed and waved his hand dismissively, as he threw the robe aside and stood. About then, Elmira came in, slightly flushed, in her black dress, with her gray hair neatly braided on top of her head. She took both her husband's hands in hers. She kissed him on the cheek before turning to her visitors. She greeted Lucas with a cheerful hallo and spoke to Angus more specifically.

"Ah, Lucas, young man. I see you've chosen to visit my home. I've been waiting to see you again. Mr. Meldrick, I'm so pleased to see you. Are you hungry? Not to worry, I have a nice dinner prepared, and we'll eat soon." She leaned down to the boy's level and said with a conspiratorial wink, "In the meantime, why don't you go with Anita and see the kittens in the kitchen while your father and I talk? Would you like that?" The boy's eyes brightened, and he nodded his head.

"Anita, you can come out of hiding now." The maid who had answered the door peered around the corner of the wall and came into the room.

"Señora? You call me?" She blushed, her ears turning pink.

"Yes, I did, you naughty girl. Please take Lucas to see the kittens, and I'll call you when we're finished." The girl left the room with a suddenly shy boy in tow. He looked back to see if his Angus approved and received a nod and smile. He turned and skipped away, leaving a moment of awkwardness behind.

"She's a great gossip and likes to hear what my guests have to say so she can tell her mother. She was listening around the corner. They're a poor family, and she has several younger siblings. She means no harm, and I'll miss her; she's such a comfort when I'm feeling lonely and melancholy. Now, you didn't come to talk about my servants." She smiled and began to discuss the trip to Missouri and how she could help with the boy's personal needs and education.

"You don't need to worry about expenses, Meldrick," Pulaski added to his wife's words. "The colonel explained about your position as supply wagon driver. We have our own carriage and driver. Young Juan Cortez will see to my needs on the trail. We'll be one happy family, right?"

With the mention of a wagon driver, questions spurted from Angus' mouth. "Has the carriage been caulked to keep the water out? Are you using mules or horses?"

"Very good, my man. I see you are a person who thinks of practical things. That's impressive. You told me, Mira, that this would be a good man to look out after us. My lingering doubts are assuaged."

"Ignore Tom." Mrs. Pulaski gazed at her husband with a tolerant smile. "He likes to tease, and he means nothing of it. Our carriage is of good quality and will survive the passage with few issues, if God is with us."

The men discussed the details of the trip, while Elmira sat quietly listening, putting in a word here or there when it suited her. Angus had no experience hiring a nursemaid, so he told of what he had observed of the boy on the trail to Santa Fe. In the intimacy of the tent and wagon, he knew what was required of a six-year-old boy. He knew little about teaching his letters and numbers, he told her, and he felt the boy had suffered there. He shared what little he'd been able to teach him, that he could mark some letters and spell his name both on paper and in the sand.

In about thirty minutes, the maid returned, and Lucas was bright-eyed with the kittens.

"What did you think of my little pets?" Mrs. Pulaski motioned the boy to her, and she smiled at him.

"They're funny. Do they always make squeaky noises? One licked me on the face. I think it liked me."

"I'm sure it did. Let's go see about our meal. I'm certain you must be a hungry little boy, and I know I'm hungry. Mr. Pulaski was telling me earlier that if lunch didn't hurry up, he might be hungry enough to eat a little boy or two."

Lucas' eyes grew wide, and Tom Pulaski called out, "Wait a minute, Mira. I said no such thing . . ."

"But then," and she touched Lucas on the nose with the tip of one finger, "he always likes to tease, and he never means a word of it."

Pulaski laughed with his wife, and he rubbed the boy's hair as they headed into the dining room. They sat down to a well-cooked meal of boiled beef, roasted corn, peas, rice and hot yeast bread. Angus' eyes opened wide; he'd seen only the flat round cakes served since he'd arrived in Santa Fe. Of course, the Army cook baked yeast bread, but it wasn't soft on the inside with a slightly crusty outside like the civilians enjoyed. For dessert, there were slices of peaches covered with clotted cream. They said a cordial farewell, and Lucas talked of the kittens all the way to the camp. Angus put him down for a short nap; his eyes were drooping with fatigue.

*****

The next time Angus encountered Mrs. Pulaski in town, she was sitting under a shade tree on the plaza, with some of her friends.

"Ah, Mr. Meldrick. You must let me introduce you."

"Mrs. Pulaski." He removed his hat, held it behind his back, and bowed slightly at the waist.

"This is Mrs. Carlos Ramirez, Mrs. Jeremiah Hale,

Mrs. Winona Rodgers and Miss Cimmie Rodgers. Ladies, this is the gentleman I told you about who will be delivering us back to our home in Missouri. He and his son joined us for the most charming lunch just a week ago, and I'm certain I could have no finer protector for our travels through Indian territory."

"Ma'am, ma'am." He nodded to the ladies before replacing his hat. He had been introduced as though he were a gentleman from the East, and he carried his head a little higher. One of the ladies was dark-haired and wore a mantilla on her head. She carried a fan which she waved in front of her flirtatiously, but he looked past the sparkle in her eyes. He excused himself and went on his way, stopping at a general store. There were so many things he needed to buy for the boy: a heavy winter coat, some undergarments, a small slate and chalk for his schooling and new shoes. He greeted the proprietor, who spoke little English and smiled at him with yellowed, tobacco-stained teeth and a weather-beaten, pitted face. After studying the quality of the children's clothing and seeing the prices marked on each item, he shook his head and turned aside. The door shut gently behind him.

— 7 —

They stayed in Santa Fe for a couple of weeks, getting outfitted for the return trip. Angus found time to visit with one of the merchants he had become acquainted with on the route south, Eldrod Carter. He had two boys, and Lucas had a chance to play with them, skipping and running like wild Indians. His wife was a pleasant woman, and when he mentioned that Elmira was taking the boy under her wing on the trip to Jefferson Barracks, she gave him the name of a priest who had tutored her boys for a while and who was an expert in the Shakespearean prose of England. Angus had very little education himself and couldn't see a need for Lucas to learn about Shakespeare, but he wished them well on their journey to Chihuahua. He had several Army friends, and he and the boy talked with them in the evenings, often playing a few hands of poker while Lucas slept on a blanket nearby. He took his mules to the farrier for new shoes, and he stopped at a leather goods shop for repairs on his frayed holster. He and the boy spent a Sunday night with the Pulaski family, and Angus shared how impressed he was with the quality and quantity of food displayed on the table.

When he was searching in the bottom of the boy's trunk to see if there was something he could sell in the town for extra money, he found a daguerreotype of Adam Griswold in his Army uniform and a second likeness of the family when Lucas was about two years old, sitting in his mother's lap, his father standing behind the woman, his hand on her shoulder. The woman was beautiful; her eyes seemed luminous and her skin clear. He looked at the images for a long time. The man was thin of face with slightly protruding ears. His hair appeared dark, and the color of his eyes might be blue or gray, though the metallic image made it impossible to tell. There was a resemblance in Lucas, one that would appear more so when he was older. Angus rewrapped the metal photographs and the other items in the cloth, placed them in the bottom of the trunk and packed the rest of their possessions on top.

He picked up the carpetbag that Mrs. Griswold had carried on the boat from Natchez, planning to stuff it with a few of the lad's clothes to be carried in the wagon under the seat. As he was running his hand along the edge of the bag, looking for a lost sock or cap, he heard something tinkle. He felt of the soft, velvety material, and his fingers encountered something hard, something thin and round.

He made a small slit in the cloth with his knife and looked inside. He gasped as silver and gold coins came pouring out of the opening, one twenty-dollar gold piece and two silver dollar pieces, a number of smaller coins and several bills in Army script, evidently put there by the aunt or maybe Adam Griswold for the support of his wife.

He sat on his haunches and stared. Then he began to laugh. The bonus find was enough to buy the boy a coat and shoes, with a few extras besides. He stuffed a couple of paper bills in his pocket and returned the rest to the carpetbag, using his needle and thread to stitch it neatly in place. He filled the bag with the boy's change of clothes, an extra pair of shoes, his own personal items, and took a stroll of the grounds to calm his nerves, with a smile on his face.

*****

Angus asked Zellers to mind the boy and went into town. He visited an establishment reported to be clean and honest, and popular with the troopers, but his call on the woman left him feeling dry and empty; still, he drank several glasses of cheap liquor until his head was swimming and went upstairs again. He stumbled back to camp and, after passing a coin to Zellers, crawled into the tent and lay for hours, sleepless with the predicament into which the colonel had trapped him.

On a cool, hazy morning just as the sun began to rise, Angus dressed himself and the boy, ate breakfast and took Lucas to see the fiesta. The colorful banners hanging on cords from pole to pole across the plaza, and the life-like posters in the windows and on sides of buildings, had been up since the first day they arrived announcing Saints Day, with a parade and an afternoon bull fight, culminating that night with fireworks and a dance on the plaza. The bullfighting and the dancing weren't appropriate for a six-year-old boy, but the parade and fireworks could be exciting. He walked with the boy's hand in his to the edge of the crowd. Lucas grew timid with the large number of people, so Angus boosted him onto his shoulders, causing his hat to hang on the cord behind his neck. The smell of frying onions, cinnamon, roasted meat and green peppers mingled and tempted the senses as they took their places at the front of the audience. The music came first. A group of men dressed in red suits with tambourines, fiddles, guitars and clanging bells marched down the street ahead of the procession. Men were dressed in strange costumes, and women displayed painted faces, shiny red and stark white like flour paste; and he held on tightly to Lucas.

The boy's eyes grew bright and glowing, and he squealed with delight. There were clowns and streamers, and mischievous boys running through the crowd with sticks shooting sparks of fire into the air and setting off fire bombs that made loud popping sounds, which made Lucas cringe, but Angus explained that they were not to harm him. The boy pointed to the string of lights in candle boxes hanging on the poles and trailing rockets flashing in the sky. The bells from the church steeple rang out loud and clear in the crisp air. But, the best of all the sights and sounds was the men carrying the statue of Madonna through the streets with poles on their shoulders. Angus felt a tug on his hair, and he set the boy down where he jumped up and down and screamed, "Mama! Mama!" Angus didn't correct him and noticed that the image on the plastered doll face did somewhat resemble the woman in the portrait. After the parade, he took him to a vendor's booth and bought some folded flat cakes filled with peppery, spiced beans. Angus gave him a bunch of plump purple grapes for desert. The boy was exhausted, and he carried him home.

Rising early as was his custom, Angus stayed near his wagon, awaiting orders. After breakfast, he dipped the bucket into the river and heated the water for baths for himself and the boy. He scrounged in the old trunk and found their clean and mended drawers and outer garments. The boy howled with protest when he scrubbed his ears and neck, but Angus talked to him softly, and he calmed. He told the boy to practice his letters and numbers on his tablet in the wagon, while he bathed himself in the tent. It was an awkward attempt, stooping and almost tripping while he lifted first one leg and then the other, with nothing to hold him steady. He moved like a man refreshed when he donned the clean clothes. Afterwards, he poured out the used and stained water. He checked on Lucas and heated another bucketful of the cold, clear liquid. He sat on his lone rock and washed their clothes, and then he strung them on a cord tied to the tent pole and a scrawny willow tree trunk. They flapped in the breeze and sunshine while he attended to some other chores around the camp. He picked up some fallen limbs from the trees along the banks and heard a splash in the water. From the uniforms strewn across the smaller shrubs, it was several soldiers taking a swim. It would have been easier than his own crude method of bathing.

He wandered over where he could see that some of the men had lingered after breakfast at the cook's tables to play parlor games: jackstraws, Draughts, Teetotum, the ever-present poker, and the new game called Mansion of Happiness. He hadn't played it, but it was popular among the officers. He lazily watched at the table for a while and returned to his own camp.

From a distance, he could hear the troopers whooping and cheering as they held a wrestling match. He couldn't see the activity, but it was loud enough for him to know someone would end up with a bloody nose and bruised knuckles, not to mention the stiffened muscles and strained backs.

Claymore passed by his tent, and Angus called out to him, "Who won the match? Any broken bones?"

"No. Hankins won, and I lost a fiver on Silcox. That's the last time I'll bet on him; he's sluggish and won't keep his balance. It was a good match, though. Say, I've some boxes that the quartermaster sent over.

Do you have space for a few of them? He's sending more this afternoon, and I'm gettin' full up." Claymore knelt and watched as Lucas played with some baked clay marbles on the ground. He called an invitation to Angus, "They're havin' a horse race in a couple of hours; got time to come see it?"

"I'd like that, thank you. Save me a spot on the front row of spectators. Yes, bring the boxes over, if there's not more than five or six. I know we have no control over the Army supplies that we haul; the quartermaster and his underlings take care of those details. We only drive the wagons. However, I'm filled up, too, and still must make room for the lady's luggage. That's direct from the colonel, so I have to accommodate her."

Lucas gathered his marbles and put them in the cloth bag. He came to stand beside Angus. The man ruffled the boy's hair, and the child backed away, scuffing his shoes in the dirt. After a moment, Lucas returned to take his adopted father's hand.

"That American lady and her husband comin' with us on the trip? Jenkins said you'd found someone to take care of the boy. What's she like?" Claymore squinted in the sunshine, took out his handkerchief and wiped his brow. "Sure hot today."

"She's a real lady. You'll like her, I think. Name's Elmira Pulaski; her husband is one of the merchants; got sick on the way back from Chihuahua last trip, and they were stranded with no caravan going East. They'll join us on the last day. Come on. Let's get those boxes loaded so we can see the horses. How many are racing?"

They walked to Claymore's wagon, and each carried back a box and put it on the ground. While puffing and moaning, Claymore gave him more details about the race. He put down his box and went for another. He helped Angus rearrange some of the crates in the wagon, leaving the ones used by the cooks near the back so they could be easily removed when needed. Angus shifted his own things to one side, making room for Elmira's luggage. When Claymore had exchanged the three boxes from one wagon to another, he headed off for the races.

When he heard the raucous laughter and sounds of countless men gathering for an afternoon of fun, Angus called to Lucas, and holding his hand tightly in his own, walked to the flat ground selected for the horse race. Men came from all directions, hard, rough, weather-beaten-faced civilians, Dragoon officers and noncommissioned sergeants, mingling for this one time with the privates and a few women; hangers-on who followed the drum when an army was on the move. He didn't find Claymore in the crowd, but it didn't matter. He watched the horses lined up, six of them, with their riders perched on their backs, ready for the start. Bang! The starter shot off his revolver into the air, and the horses broke into a gallop down the imaginary track.

Angus watched the horsemen and glanced down at his adopted son. The boy seemed entranced by something other than the race. With a frown, he was watching a woman nearby who was leaning into the man beside her. She had on a green calico dress, with a low bodice and short blousy sleeves. There were a number of clanging bracelets on one wrist, and a shimmering necklace hung around her neck. Her face was painted a shiny red, and her hair was black as night and streaming down her back in ringlets. The man was laughing at her antics and smacked her on the lips with a kiss. She pouted and squirmed, rubbing herself against him. Angus quickly moved the boy away from the scene and walked a few yards away. The noise around him was almost deafening, and his attention was no longer on the race. With the smells and the heat, the enjoyment of the activity had evaporated.

A vendor passed with a tray hanging by leather straps from his shoulders. The tray smelled of spicy food, and Angus stopped him and bought himself and the boy a couple of folded flat cakes filled with peppers, meat and a tangy sauce. It left them thirsty, so Angus returned to his wagon to quench their thirst. He sat on his rock and, with a stick, drew an image of the woman at the track, while Lucas took a short nap in the wagon. It didn't look much like her, and he wiped the image away with his foot. The loud noise continued for another hour, and the men began walking back to their homes or tents or camps. Claymore and the cook's helper stopped by to report on how the race turned out. Angus thanked them, but his mind had already moved on. He gathered the dry clothes, folded them neatly and placed them in the trunk, took down his cord, coiled it into a small ball and put it away. Once the boy woke, Angus took his pen knife from his pocket and showed Lucas how to whittle with a small block of wood from a cottonwood tree that had fallen beside the stream. In a few minutes, a pile of shavings appeared beside his rock, and he picked them up and threw them into the fire, making it flare and blaze up. He handed Lucas the crude shape of a horse he had carved, and the boy ran about the camp pretending it was a race horse.

Angus forwent the usual Army meal to go into town. He wouldn't have many chances to eat restaurant food before they arrived back in Missouri. He walked slowly so the boy could keep up, but grew impatient and hoisted him onto his shoulders. The boy held his carved racing horse in his hand and twirled it around, bouncing on Angus' shoulders. Angus put him back down and smiled. He teased the boy about his horse and started making funny faces and neighing like a horse. The boy screamed with joy, and they raced for a few steps, with the large man suiting his pace to the shorter legs of his competition. He sobered when he came to the gate of the city. The sun was beginning to sink low on the horizon, and a bright light shone on the opposing adobe dwellings and buildings of the plaza.

He searched until he saw a building with the word Café and held the door for Lucas. The inside of the building was dim with candles in sconces along the walls and on the tables. It looked clean, and he saw a few families seated at the tables, so he decided it was a good place to bring the boy. They were seated by a pretty senorita in a bright red, yellow, green and blue dress, with jangling bracelets on her wrists. He ordered a simple meal of soup and flat cakes, not too spicy for the boy, and it was soon brought to them. He looked at the paintings on the walls of bullfighters and sleepy-looking haciendas with tall trees and flowered bushes, places that represented where the rich grandees had lived when the Spanish ruled Mexico. When the boy had finished and started squirming in his seat, he paid for the meal and walked outside.

The bell was chiming in the church steeple, and something seemed to draw him in that direction. He saw a black-clad woman enter, her head covered with a mantilla and coral comb, and he stepped inside. The boy tugged at his hand, but he led him to a seat at the back without speaking. Lucas sat beside him and looked with interest at the painted statue of the Madonna and child. The silence was soothing after the noise of the outside world. There were dozens of lighted tapers around the altar railing and in small glass jars on a table. He saw the woman kneel and make the sign of the cross, then take a seat in the silent, almost dim space. He bowed his head, but no prayer came to him. He sat still and watched as the woman rose and went to the altar. She took one of the tapers and lit one of the smaller candles in a glass jar. She bowed and crossed herself again, and slowly walked down the aisle and out the door. Without thinking about what he was doing, Angus rose and mimicked her actions, and he smiled at Lucas as he looked inquiringly at him. He placed an American coin in the poor box and walked outside.

He took a deep breath of the bracing air. The sun was hidden by the buildings, and he could see the shadows were long and the day was quickly fading into night. He heard a sound and turned. It was the black-clad woman, standing in the shadows of the church portal.

"Sir," she said. "Are you Angus Meldrick?"

"Yes, I'm Meldrick." He couldn't see her face for the dark netting. She had a heavy French accent and a soft, sweet cadence in her voice, belying his original estimate of her origins. He glanced at Lucas, who was kicking up dust with his feet.

"I'm Dona Maria Fortunado. I am an acquaintance of the American lady, Elmira Pulaski. She said you have been kind enough to take her back to her country. This is so?"

"Yes, it's so. We'll travel with the caravan and the soldiers from the encampment. How may I help you?"

"Oh, it is not for that reason that I stopped you, sir. I need no help; I have my family with me. But to tell you I am charmed by your so kind offer for my friend. She has not been comfortable in this alien world since her husband became ill. She misses her own daughters and grandchildren. I have said a prayer to the blessed Virgin for your safe journey. Is this your boy?"

"Yes, he's my son," he said with pride and smiled at the sleepy boy, standing as still as stone, the race

116

horse clutched tightly in his hand.

"I shall let you go on your way, Mr. Meldrick. May the good Mother of God protect you on your journey. Good night." She was gone with a whisper of skirts and the faint pungent scent of incense.

Angus turned toward the Army encampment, his mind in a whirl of sensations: the church, the candles, the woman and her prayers. He picked up the boy and carried him. He was soon fast asleep, the carved horse still clutched in his hand on his chest. He saw the glow of the campfires, and they guided his footsteps until he was in the familiar setting near the wagons. He could smell the remains of the evening meal, and the cook and his helpers were clearing the tables. There was a light in the hospital tent, perhaps someone injured at the wrestling match or the horse race. He put Lucas to bed inside the tent and removed the boy's shoes. He took off his hat and sat on the cot beside his son watching him sleep. With a sigh he rose and checked the wagon and found that the cook's helpers had fastened the canvas cover ties securely. He made sure his fire was dead in the pit. He sat on the rock for a while and watched the activity at the cook's tent. His eyes grew heavy, and he entered his tent and went to sleep.

*****

On the day before they were to leave, a Mexican boy of about twelve brought him a note sealed with a wax stamp. He gave him a coin, and he scampered off in a hurry. Angus looked at the paper, turning it over and over. It was unmarked on the outside. He ran his fingernail along the seal, and it snapped open.

"Dear Mr. Meldrick, I would like for you to be my guest at the Alcalde's house for dinner at eight o'clock. Please dress as formally as you can. E. Pulaski."

Angus folded the note and gazed at the horizon. He glanced at his trousers, brushed them with the flat of his hand and watched the dust fly. He opened the note again, reading . . . *guest* . . . *at the alcalde's house*. His eyes reread the words several times, as a bemused expression crossed his face, and he adjusted his shirt as if he could make the worn fabric more presentable in the futile motion. He called to Lucas who was sitting on the ground making circles and lines in the dirt that were supposed to resemble the alphabet, but still had some practice to be done on them.

"Let's go, son."

The boy rose, and they started walking; Lucas kept his stick in his hand and waved it around like it was a sword, mimicking the officers practicing their swordplay. Angus found Private Zellers standing with a few other Dragoons near the baker's wagon. The pleasant smell of cake baking teased his nostrils as he passed the temporary bakery.

"Zellers!" he called out. The clink of horseshoes in the air revealed the pastime that occupied them. The private separated himself from the group. He glanced at Lucas.

"Yes, sir?" and he looked back longingly toward his fellow game players.

"Are you free tonight to watch the boy? I'll give you a buck. I've been invited to dinner with the Mexican society. From say seven-fifteen to ten of the clock?"

"Yeh, I guess so. At your wagon?" The horseshoes clinked once again, and one of the Army men called to Zellers, asking him if he intended to withdraw from the game. If not, it was his turn.

"That's fine, then. I see your friends need your attention. I'll expect you at seven fifteen of the clock."

"Thank you, Mr. Meldrick. I'll be prompt."

Angus nodded and stood for another moment as he watched Zellers run off to his friends. He no longer had time for the games of chance he'd participated in at one time when he was younger. He clasped the boy around the shoulders, smiled at him and asked him if he had the energy to race back to their camp. At the wagon, he dug out his best suit and white shirt from the trunk where he had packed them. The shirt was wrinkled but clean; the coat was getting a little tight through the shoulders, but he could still wear it. He removed them until time to get ready, took out a small cloth and began to shine his store-bought shoes. When he had finished, he took a bucket and dipped some water out of the river. The boy had gone to sleep in the shade of the wagon. He checked that he was alright and began to prepare for his big night in the town. He saw from the corner of his eyes a furry creature speed out of sight. It looked like a rat. He could tolerate spiders and insects, but the tiny rodents with long skinny tails gave him a fright.

*****

"Mr. Meldrick? It's Private Zellers. I'm a few minutes ahead of schedule, but I thought you might like to get away a bit early." He stood politely outside the tent, waiting for Angus' response. Lucas came bursting forth instead, energetic with enthusiasm after his short nap.

"Mr. Jimmy, did you come to play?" The boy grabbed his hand and made to pull him into the tent, but Angus moved the flap aside and stopped him with a laugh.

"The boy seems to enjoy your company. I expect you'll keep him occupied during the evening. Give me a few minutes, and I'll be away." Angus' shirt was still undone, and he withdrew back into the tent.

"He'll keep *me* occupied," Zellers called after him with a grin. He knelt to Lucas, holding out his hand to shake. "Give me one there, partner. This is your promise of good behavior, tonight."

"I'll be good," and Lucas grinned, "if you get me a piece of cake."

"I heard that." Angus pulled the flap aside, and he poked his head through. "No such deals, son. I'm onto you, now."

Zellers gave Lucas a sad face, then he laughed,

stood and took the boy's hand, leading him to a stunted tree, where he broke off two short branches so they could begin a game of mock sword play.

At fifteen minutes past seven of the clock, Angus Meldrick, spruced up in his city clothes, and with shiny shoes, hugged the boy, cautioned Zellers against letting the boy out of his sight, and left his wagon and headed the short distance to the gates of Santa Fe. He waved at the guards and strolled to the house of the alcalde, where he showed his invitation to the strong-armed man at the door, who took his hat and placed it beside a dozen others on a table nearby. He pulled his cloth from an inner pocket and stooped to put a new shine on his shoes. He walked down a long hall until he heard voices and walked to the open door. A guard in red and gold livery stood at attention at the door and only nodded when he pulled out his invitation again and showed it to him.

He needn't have worried about his reception, for he was hailed immediately by a couple of lieutenants of the Dragoons and their wives.

"Mr. Meldrick, I'm pleased to see you here." Prunella, the wife of Lt. Gregory Forsyth, waved her kerchief at him.

"Yes, Angus. You must come speak with us. We've never seen you so gussied up. This is a treat for eyes all around." The gibe was from Lt. Packard. As the colonel's adjutant, he was highly placed and a fixture in demand at community social events.

Angus joined them and spoke politely for a few

moments. "I'm a bit nervous. My invitation is from Elmira Pulaski, the American woman who'll be traveling with us in the caravan. I've yet to find her or her husband, Tom. She asked me to wear my best, but I can see now that I'm far from adequately done up." His eyes searched for the alcalde and saw him at the head of a table with his staff of office in his hand. Mrs. Pulaski and several ladies were conversing nearby.

"You're fine," said Packard. "Simply smile a lot and laugh at the jokes, and everyone will think you're wonderful."

A Mexican merchant's woman tapped his arm with her fan, folded into a stiff column. "My name is Sonia Rodriguez. We are pleased to have the Americans here tonight to join us in our simple supper."

A man leaned around her and held out his arm to shake. "Welcome, Meldrick. Name's Reynaldo. So glad you could come. Sonia is my wife."

"Ah. I'm pleased to meet your wife. She is very gracious."

After a few more minutes of congratulatory conversation, Angus excused himself and walked toward the ladies. He was a few feet away when Elmira came toward him, her hair coiffured high on her head with a white feather of some sort and a couple of curls behind one ear. She had on a deep purple dress and a small bag hung by a chain from one wrist. He looked for Tom Pulaski but didn't see him.

"Angus, please come and meet my friends. I'm so glad you came out tonight. I wasn't sure that you would." She glanced behind him. "You didn't bring the boy? Oh, I hoped you would. I wanted to introduce my new charge to the alcalde's wife. Well, no matter." She slipped her hand inside his elbow and led him to the ladies.

"Where is your husband tonight, ma'am?" He barely had time to get out the words as they traversed the floor.

He heard her faintly whisper, "The party is too big a strain on his nerves, and he's gone to bed early."

For Angus, the party went downhill from there. He was in high above his rank and social order. He had met two of the women while sitting with Elmira that day in the plaza, but their husbands' faces were new to him. Carlos Ramirez and Jeremiah Hale greeted him with handshakes. They sat at a long table, in a room filled with tapers of beeswax that flickered and cast ghostly shadows into the corners. Elmira sat on his right, giving him one person to converse with, for the matronly lady in low-cut lace and satin on his left spoke only Spanish, and he understood only one word in ten.

Captain Nelson, whom Angus hadn't seen until they were seated, was across from him. The man seemed very amiable to those of high social status on either side of him, but when he greeted Angus, his words were those of a superior for a hired man. Liveried footmen brought bowls of spicy soup and platters of roasted meat; and dishes of squash, corn, beans and boiled eggs.

"Mr. Meldrick, you do enjoy meat?" Mrs. Pulaski lifted a large fork, and she speared a section of roasted flesh. She lifted it and brought it to his plate, holding it hovering in the air.

"Yes, thank you." He smiled at her and raised his plate a few inches to accept the steaming food.

"Help yourself to anything you want. No one will force you, but it's good manners to sample each item. Eat hearty. There's plenty all around."

Soon there followed a large crockery platter of fresh peaches, melons and purple grapes; and when it seemed there couldn't possibly be more food, there were small bowls of boiled milk with the taste of cinnamon and nutmeg. The women left the room, and the men sat and talked while puffing on their cigaritas or pipes. The smoke encircled their heads like a fog. At last, the alcalde rose from the table, and the other officials and guests followed him into a huge hollow room, where in a corner a band of guitars, violins and a single fife played loud, cheerful music.

Angus was hard pressed to remember everyone's name. He spoke for several minutes with the alcalde and his gracious wife, and with the colonel, who sent him a knowing wink, bringing panic to the freight driver's face. Angus greeted Dona Maria Fortunado, and she introduced him to her husband, dressed in sober black with embroidered gold trim on his jacket. His level of dress indicated he could well be a city official or wealthy merchant. They didn't speak of the meeting at the church. Elmira stayed by his side most of the time, except when he was conversing with his officer friends about the trail back to Missouri, and the mention of bandits was heard, in which she quietly slipped away and left them to their conversation. Angus' face became flushed and his words thick from the unaccustomed champagne and rich food. There was one lady who kept eyeing him askance, and he finally decided to approach her.

"Good evening, ma'am, I don't remember if we've been introduced. I'm Angus Meldrick." He bowed politely.

"Oh, I know who you are, Mr. Meldrick. I'm Norbetta Simmons. I heard from the surgeon of Lieutenant Selwig's death, from snake bite, he said. He was a particular friend of mine. How sad, but so common in these parts. I'm with the Mexican caravan parked outside the town. My husband is over there drinking himself into a stupor." She pointed to a heavy-set man with a black beard and bushy eyebrows. The woman was at least twenty years younger than her husband, and rather stout, herself.

"Ah, I know your husband from a distance, though I don't think we've met. You came with us from Missouri, I believe. Zariah is your husband's name, if I remember correctly." Angus watched while the man drank from a small crystal glass and caught another as a waiter passed by. He was involved in an intense conversation with two other men, and they held crystal glasses of their own. "I hadn't realized he was married. I apologize for the oversight."

She opened her fan and gazed at him provocatively over the top. "I thought about speaking with you a few times but was discouraged by the other ladies in the train. They thought it would cause a scandal, my talking to a bachelor." The woman looked at him questioningly.

"I don't know about that." Angus shrugged. "I suppose it might in some circles."

"I was at Jefferson Barracks when they brought Adam Griswold's body to the camp. The boy is his son, I believe?"

"Yes, ma'am. Lieutenant Adam Griswold." Angus cast his eyes about the room, looking for Elmira, but he didn't see her in the crowd.

"I heard about the fight in the saloon. It wasn't quite like the rumors suggest, was it?"

Angus turned and looked more sharply at his interrogator. "Where did you hear that? What do you know?"

"My husband was at the saloon that night. He told me about it. He said it was all quite a tragic mistake. Lieutenant Griswold being shot, I mean, and that rumor about the saloon girl, Lily." Mrs. Simmons glanced down, with a superior smirk on her face. She cleared her expression before looking up to find Angus' eyes once again.

"Damn," Angus muttered. Then louder, he replied to the lady with a harsher voice than he normally would use to speak to a woman, revealing the measure of how upset her revelation made him. "Why didn't your husband come to me on the road from St. Louis? Here we are hundreds of miles from Sheriff Terrill and his authority. There was plenty of opportunity during the transport of the train across the country."

"Oh, I don't know about that," she said with nonchalance. "It's all my husband's business."

"Did he talk to the sheriff about that night?" He held his breath for an answer.

"Yes, he spoke up at the inquest later, too. I was in attendance in the audience. It was an amazing sight; I'd never been in a courtroom before." She smiled at the remembrance.

"I can't place the inquest and want to know more about it. If you don't mind, ma'am, I'd like to speak to your husband." Without giving her a chance to refuse, he took her arm rather roughly and led her to the man who was drinking so heavily. He burst rudely into the conversation of the three men, breaking off their words in mid-sentence.

"Mr. Simmons, I need to speak with you outside a moment."

All the men looked at him as though he had sprouted two heads. Mr. Simmons turned to him with a somewhat jaundiced slur to his speech.

"Angus Meldrick? The freight driver for the army?" Without waiting for an answer, he turned to his wife. "Norbetta, what've you done? Of course, sir, I'll speak with you. Excuse us, gentlemen. It seems I have pressing business elsewhere." He bowed to the other men and placed his half-empty glass on a nearby table.

The three of them walked toward the exit to the room.

The guard at the door saluted them as they passed by and watched as they walked down the hallway a few steps. Their footsteps rang in the cathedral silence of the long passageway. Words were being exchanged between husband and wife, with the man berating his wife for instigating trouble with her gossip of things long past and better forgotten among the public spectators.

"Sir." Angus stopped and turned to the man, who was swaying on his feet. "Your wife says you testified at the inquest into Lieutenant Griswold's death at Slim's saloon at St. Louis. Is this true? What did you see that night?"

Simmons blinked a few times. His wife stood by and shivered in the slightly cool air of the room. She pulled her shawl more closely around her shoulders. After a few moments of unfocused attempts at concentration, the man's expression cleared, and he began to speak.

"Yes, I was there that night, and I testified at Sheriff Terrill's inquest. I told Norbetta not to say anything to you; but she has always been impulsive and quick to jump into situations that don't concern her." He sighed and straightened his spine.

"That may be, sir, but the matter's been broached, and it can't be put back in the bottle. Tell me what you know."

"Those rumors about the lieutenant weren't true. The rumors about his involvement with the saloon gal,

Lily, that is. I saw Lt. Griswold the day before he was struck down by that coward and thief, Garland. We had a meal together, and he was asking about a room at a boarding house or hotel for his aunt and son, who were coming in on a steamer from Natchez. I don't figure a man waiting anxiously for his son to join him would be messing around with a saloon girl, and I told the sheriff. I understand his wife had recently died."

"What happened at the inquest? I didn't know they had held one; I was busy with my chores at the Barracks, and I had recently arrived in town, after the saloon brawl. I supposed someone would inform me of the outcome of the business, but no one ever came to me." Angus huffed out his cheeks. "I'm surprised my friend Sheriff Wade Terrill didn't contact me."

"I guess everyone thought with taking the boy in tow, that you weren't interested in the outcome. The coroner ruled it a death by mischief, by person or persons unknown, but everyone who was there knew well who done it. Judge Maddock even testified, and we all know he's as honest as a man can be and stand on two feet. I'm sorry if you weren't told. If I'd known, I'd spoke to you on the train. I saw you and the boy with the army encampment. I got the impression you were happy with your new family and had left the past behind you in the city. You going to keep the boy?"

Simmons asked the question with a tone of genuine concern. Norbetta drew her handkerchief from her bag and sniffed in sympathy.

"Yes, I intend to keep him, if possible. I've grown

to enjoy his company. He's a delightful boy. I thank you for the information, Mr. Simmons. The people were mistaken in their judgment. I'm very interested in learning about the truth, for the boy's sake."

Norbetta sniffed again. "I'm sorry we didn't approach you earlier, Mr. Meldrick. I suppose you'll be going back to St. Louis with the Dragoons?" She asked the question with a speculative gleam in her eyes.

"Thank you, Mrs. Simmons, you are so kind. Yes, I'll return with the boy to my position at Jefferson Barracks. I've hired Mrs. Elmira Pulaski to accompany us and care for the boy when I'm about my duties. She's inside now. Have you met her? No? Then, please come into the room and I'll introduce you. Are you going on to Chihuahua, Mr. Simmons?" Angus was still terse, but his emotions were firmly intact as he conversed with the merchant and led them to the group surrounding Elmira. He kept a smile and a pleasant countenance on his face; discussed the trip south with the merchants and soldiers; and finally left to attend his own business, after assuring Elmira he would pick up her, Pulaski and their luggage very early on the morrow.

Leaving the alcalde's house, the streets were dark; there were no public lights to guide him, only a few lighted windows projecting soft beams of illumination onto the dusty street. In one dwelling across the street, the silhouette of a woman on the shade suggested hopes and dreams of a family for whoever lived inside.

He stopped for a moment and watched until she moved away. He was startled by the closing of a door, and he moved on down the street, his stride lengthening as he saw the twinkling lights of campfires in the distance. He stumbled once on the path to his wagon, his concentration centered on what he had heard from the couple. He paid Private Zellers and sent him on his way. The boy was asleep in his place in the tent. He pulled the covers over his shoulders and leaned over to give him a gentle kiss on the forehead.

Angus stirred the coals of his small campfire and sat alone in the night staring at the flames. His haunted eyes revealed his doubts in how he'd handled his part in taking the boy. He whispered his thoughts to the flames, to let them rise into the night sky and disappear into the air, forgotten by anyone except him.

"Would it have made a difference if I'd waited until after the inquest to take the boy? The child's aunt was so adamant that she didn't want him. That first day of our meeting at the steamer pier and learning of the saloon brawl that had resulted in the lieutenant's death. Maybe, it's best that I accepted the invitation from Elmira to the alcalde's dinner. Now, I can put the past behind me until I arrive back in the city and can approach Sheriff Terrill about the inquest. Will they try to take the boy from me?"

He threw sand on his fire and crawled into the tent with his son. Fully dressed, he wrapped his arms around the boy and pulled the blankets over his head. He whispered into the darkness, "Tomorrow will start a new chapter in my life." Then he smiled and murmured, "Zariah Simmons pouring champagne down his gullet as though it were water. The man will have a terrible headache in the morning."

— 8 —

Angus was awakened by the stirrings of the men at the wagons near him and crawled out of his blankets. He stretched high to the sky and bent over to get the kinks out of his back. The boy was still sleeping, and he roused him gently and carried him to the wagon, so he could take down the tent. He yawned. The air was crisp and clear. There were still stars, although a faint light could be seen on the eastern horizon. He removed the pole, and the tent tumbled into an ungainly heap. He carefully rolled it and placed it inside the wagon and stuffed the pole and stakes into a canvas bag and laid them near it. Next, he made sure he had his kettle, cups, spoon and all other equipment inside the wooden box. The light was so dim he stumbled over a rock and caught himself before he fell. He went to the rope corral and selected six mules; the animals were shared among the various wagons, so he didn't have to see that he got certain ones each morning. The cook's helper was in the corral, and they greeted each other. He walked the mules to the wagon and hitched them to the yoke. When he finished, he made sure the canvas top of the wagon was tied securely, and heaving a sigh of resignation, drove the mules out of line and toward the gates of the city.

He answered the sleepy challenge from the guardhouse and drove through the streets until he came to the home of Tom and Elmira Pulaski. There were lights on in the house, telling that they were up and prepared for the trip, as he'd asked them to be. He knocked sharply on the door, and a Mexican girl in a calico dress answered it.

"Please to come in," she invited in a heavy Spanish accent.

"Thank you, miss. It's very early. Are you entirely awake?" He smiled at her.

"You're very welcome. Thank you for asking. Yes, it is early, and I am awake. I am sorry to see Señor and Señora Pulaski leave. With them goes my work. But, what to do?" She shrugged and stepped aside.

Angus removed his hat and stepped inside the room. He looked around at the crates and boxes and trunk. There was more luggage than the Pulaskis had indicated they would be transporting. He turned when he heard a sound come from behind him.

"Good morning, Angus. I trust you slept well." Elmira, dressed again in black, with a wide-brimmed hat on her head, with netting across the face, stepped into the room. Her eyes were barely visible through the heavy cloth, but her voice sparkled with excitement. She didn't wait for an answer but started speaking in fluent Spanish to the girl, who rushed out of the room on some errand. Tom Pulaski came from a back room, dressed in a black suit, with heavy boots on his feet, his trousers stuffed into the top. They shook hands, and Angus turned to the woman as she spoke.

"Take the trunk out first; it's the heaviest. Then we'll see to the crates and boxes. I'll help with the lighter ones." Elmira wrinkled her nose and frowned. With the authority of a general, she ordered him around, until the whole of the luggage was snug in the back of his freight wagon. He had to shift some things to better distribute the weight, and Lucas raised his head at the disturbance.

"Hello, Lucas. I'm sorry to disturb your sleep." Angus reached to his face and pressed his palm against the soft cheek, still warm from sleep and not fully awake.

"Go back to sleep, child. It's not yet morning, and you need your rest." Mrs. Pulaski leaned into the wagon and comforted him.

"Mama?"

"No, darling child, it's Aunt Elmira. We're going on a long trip together, you and me and your papa. It'll be such fun that you won't notice the distance. Come down now and visit the necessary, if you need, before we leave."

"Okay." He pushed the covers aside and began to wriggle free.

She helped him down from the wagon, while Angus adjusted the canvas over the vehicle. As he waited on Lucas, Angus began checking the cords holding the luggage secure. Pulaski joined him, and a young Mexican man drove up in a black carriage, its wheels painted yellow, sporting a heavy leather cover and wide seat. The man dropped from the carriage and tied the reins to the post.

"My driver, Meldrick. Juan Cortez. He'll follow your lead, of course. He's a fine fellow but understands very little English."

Angus shook hands and smiled at the man, not knowing what else to do. He finished tying the cords to hold the luggage in place and turned to see the maid return with a basket on her arm and a coffee pot in her hand, bringing with it the aroma of coffee and spices. He took a deep breath and sighed. She curtsied and returned to the house. He raised the cloth on the basket and saw warm sweet buns, almost dripping with honey. He remarked to Pulaski, "They must have been up early indeed to have baked such a treat."

"Aye, the household's been alive since the small hours. We knew we must be ready when you arrived."

The sun peeped over the roofs of the houses as he, Pulaski, Elmira and the boy sat on the wagon seat and drank the hot, fragrant coffee and ate the buns. The maid came out with a wet cloth for them to wash their sticky fingers, took the coffee pot and cups and said something before retreating into the house. Angus knew enough Spanish to know she had said good-bye and wished them well on their journey. She closed the door gently behind her. It was the signal for Angus to drive away. Elmira chose to ride with her husband in the carriage on the first day of their journey, so she climbed down from the wagon and turned to help her husband, who growled he didn't need assistance, although he was unsteady on his feet. Angus drew the boy closer to him with an arm around his shoulders.

"Well, son, we're on our way. Just got to stop and line up with the Army wagons. Did you enjoy the sweet rolls?" He smiled and pulled the boy's coat more closely around his neck.

"Yes, Papa."

Angus smiled and straightened his shoulders. He sat more proudly as he pulled the whip from its place and released the brakes, and the mules strained against the harnesses as they began to step forward. He lightly touched a wheel-mule on its hip with his whip, and the lead mules moved faster; he had to pull tightly on the reins to slow them while on the quiet streets of the city. A few lights were burning in the windows as they left the town behind. In the morning's breeze, a banner gently undulated over the alcalde's house, and with a soft salute of one hand, Angus said his farewells to Santa Fe. He drove carefully to the army encampment and pulled the wagon to a halt to await his turn to fall in behind the lead company of Dragoons.

Cortez skillfully pulled in behind him with the

carriage. The encampment was very different from when Angus had left an hour before. The excitement was palpable, and the air was filled with familiar sounds and smells.

"Excuse me, Lucas. I'll be right back." Angus climbed down and ran to Claymore's wagon. "Heh, Clay, are you leading, or am I, today? I forgot to read the list."

"You lead, Angus; you always do. That the Pulaski carriage? I'll fall in behind it and the cook after me. Did you check your axles?" He laughed, the sound echoing through the camp like rolling thunder. Claymore was a small fellow, barely half past five feet, but he had a deep, bass voice, and strong thick arms that defied his small frame to anyone he met.

"Yes, I did. Did you?" It was a joke between the drivers, for the grease was very important to the wagons rolling though sand and dirt, being one of the main reasons wagons broke down on long, overland trips. "I tied the canvas tight, too. Don't come too close to the carriage, you old goat."

Angus swung on his heels and marched toward his own wagon, the sound of Claymore's laughter ringing in his ears. They had worked together for several years and become as close to being friends as their responsibilities allowed, traveling so much of the year.

He stopped at the carriage. "Are you ready for the road, ma'am?" He looked at the woman and smiled at her and her husband, bundled tightly in a wool rug.

"I would be much better, if you'd stop calling me

ma'am, young man. My name's Elmira. Yes, let's roll."

"Yes, Elmira," he answered meekly, and he laughed. He boarded his wagon, took a deep breath, looked at the Dragoons forming on his right and lined his wagon behind the last horses. The Army was on the march, the banners waving in the breeze, the horses slick and shiny coated, the hats snug on the top of the men's heads and the swords clapping against their sides. The line stretched for at least a mile as the formation left the city of Santa Fe behind, and Angus moved his team with his customary skill.

"Happy, Lucas?" He looked down at the boy, his eyes shining in the rays of the sun. He sat tall beside him.

"Yes, Papa."

"Jefferson Barracks, here we come!"

Angus Meldrick took the lead wagon toward the north and home. Behind the company of Dragoons, the supply wagons, the cook, hay and grain-ambulance wagon, the civilian merchants pulled out. They were followed by another company of horsemen and a limber carrying a light artillery piece. The sun shone yellow and warm as it circled the globe above them.

— 9 —

Day followed night, as the troopers and the wagons reversed the trail they had traveled the many weeks before. It became routine to the members of the parties, civilian and military alike. On and on they rolled, until they left the mountains and began to cross the prairie grasses. They left Bent's Fort behind and crossed the brackish water of the creeks and gullies and canyons. Twice it rained, and Angus was careful to secure the tent ties and the canvas of the wagon.

The morning after leaving the fort, Angus heard a great shout behind him and pulled his team to a halt. He stretched to see why Claymore had shouted and saw that his wagon was tipped at an angle. He secured the reins and jumped down. He helped Elmira and the boy down and went to assist Claymore with his wheel, but he wasn't needed. A group of Dragoons swarmed around the wagons, each volunteering advice or suggestions. Finally, one large, bold fellow simply took charge. Angus could see the stripes of a sergeant and realized why the privates backed away. He also became an observer only.

The bulky man removed the hub from the axle and pulled the wheel off. He rolled it to the side while one of the privates removed a spare from the side of the wagon. Within minutes the new wheel was on and secured, and the train was able to start again on its way. Without the help of the soldiers, Angus could see that it might have taken longer to change wheels. Later, Claymore explained that the recent dip in the river had made the wood expand, and the rim had come off. They never found the rim; it must have rolled down an incline and disappeared in the tall grass or broken soil. They hadn't stopped to look for it.

Angus dozed off and was called to attention by the sound of a woman's voice; he jerked awake, and the slight tug of his hand on the reins caused the mules to shift their weight. He had to quickly pull them into line. He looked at Elmira, to discover what had caused her to shout. She was pointing to a dancing devil in the distance, about fifty yards from the line of wagons and horsemen.

"Look, boy, what do you see?"

Lucas, who had been soundly sleeping, opened his eyes wide, unimpressed, and fidgeted on the seat. Elmira explained the swirling, rotating whirlwinds, common in the desert area, to the boy. She remarked on the distinct scent of creosote and pointed out a buzzard circling high in the sky. As he looked, it was joined by a second and a third. The birds were a sign of death: possibly an elk or rabbit.

Angus shifted on the seat, relieving some of the stiffness and ache that a long day in the wagon could create in a man's backside. He watched the riders ahead of him closely. There was an air of somnolence in the hot silence of the late afternoon wasteland.

At last, a halt was called, and the wagons drew out of line and circled around near a small stream, brown in color and deep and sluggish. There were animal tracks everywhere, soon identified as a herd of buffalo that had recently tasted the warm alkaline liquid and stirred the water with their hooves and tendency to recline and wallow in the moist earth. A few skimpy willows and cottonwoods lined the banks, but not anything thick enough to provide shade for everyone. The hard-packed earth was a reddish-brown color striated with white and yellow. Angus parked in his usual spot near the cook's wagon. The activity at the cook's wagon suggested that the food would be provided soon.

He helped Elmira down, and then Lucas. She walked a short distance, getting her bearings and helping Lucas with the laws of nature behind a scrubby oak. He turned away to prevent embarrassment and took a closer look at the landscape. Off in the distance, on the far horizon, was a long line of purple and blue hills with jagged tops; one stood taller than the rest. He laughed as Lucas came skipping back, leaving the woman a few minutes behind. She joined her husband as he began to stroll toward the captain of F Company. The man was holding up well, which was a good thing.

"Papa, Mira's going to play with me. I'm hungry." Lucas closely watched the cook in his large white apron. He had learned to recognize that it was the cook who provided him with his meal. "Will we have flat cakes and beans again?"

"I don't know, son. We'll have to wait and see." Angus smiled. The boy had grown to love the taste of the spicy Mexican food, and although it wasn't good for his young stomach, the men had saved enough green peppers to continue to serve it. It hid the taste of boiled beef from cans. He cautioned the boy not to leave the wagon, and Lucas sat in the dirt and opened his box of toy soldiers and began to play. Angus checked his mules' legs, mouths and flanks for sores or wounds from the leather straps of the harness. He looked up when he saw the woman return to the wagon.

"Are you well, Elmira?" She was walking slowly, looking at the banks of the creek. She stopped and searched the horizon for landmarks.

"I was just remembering that I know this place; I've been here before; must have been on my first trip to Mexico when I was a young bride. Do you know it?" There was a frown of concentration on her face. "I'll ask Tom when he comes back."

"I get the same feeling, like out of a dream; those striations on the banks of the creek; the line of hills in the distance."

He didn't get a chance to say more, for like the whirlwind in the desert, the colonel rode by on his large brown horse, and the dust rose around him, followed by two privates, their horses' tails flying in the air and their hooves kicking up dirt clods. Angus brought up his arm and covered his face with his sleeve to keep from choking.

"What a ruckus," Elmira said, with no humor or sympathy for the urgency of the matter. "Have they no concern for the people of the train?"

"It's the Army," Angus remarked casually. He turned and checked his wagon axles and the side boards, and the subject was dropped.

Elmira climbed into the wagon and brought out the small bag filled with beans that she had sewn and tossed it to Lucas. He wasn't able to catch it and ran to pick it up from the dirt while she was coming down. Once in his hand, he threw it at her, and it landed at her feet. It was her turn to pick it up. They went a few feet away and began to toss the bean bag back and forth. It was a pleasant sight to see them laughing and shouting and squealing with either delight or disappointment when the bag was dropped. It was too hot to continue for long; but the boy's cheeks were rosy, and his eyes sparkled with the exercise. Elmira also had moisture on her face, and she wiped it with the handkerchief from her pocket. Angus handed her a dipper of lukewarm water from the keg at the side of the wagon, and she praised him. Lucas sat down and began to play again with his toy soldiers.

Tom Pulaski returned and conversed in Spanish with Juan Cortez for a while, sitting on the ground. Pulaski had given in to the heat and discarded his heavy wrap, and the men sat in shirt sleeves and high-topped boots. Elmira joined them after a while, and since Angus didn't understand Spanish, he was excluded from the conversation. He continued his night chores, until the cook rang his bell for supper.

They learned during the late meal that one of the civilians had been thrown from his wagon and his neck was broken. His wife and children were devastated, and the colonel ordered the train stopped for a burial detail from the men in the rear company of Dragoons. It was the same type of senseless death as it had been with that of Lieutenant Jacob Selwig, sudden and unexpected. Angus' eyes were drawn to the distant hills with the news. However, the Army must continue its trek east, and the next morning, they moved out with the early sunrise.

A couple of days later, they came across the buffalo; thousands of them, they decided, between Angus and Tom Pulaski, who remarked he had never seen a herd so large. As far as the eye could see, the scraggy, heavy-coated animals covered the landscape. The Army column had no choice but to wait until they rumbled out of sight. A few daring shooters brought down a half dozen, and they had fresh meat for several days, soup made of hump ribs, and pemmican for the rest of the trip. It was a welcome treat to their jaded taste buds, for the green Mexican peppers had run out weeks before. The popping sounds in the distance indicated the civilians had brought down more than the Army. Fires were built in pits, and stretched out on ropes, the meat smoked to perfection; the smell assailed the senses. Angus estimated the camp at about fifteen miles from Pawnee Creek, but when he asked a lieutenant the distance, he was told it was farther.

Antelope were sighted on the left, and but for the full complement of buffalo meat, riders would have taken after them. The wagons were packed with the pemmican, and empty tins had been filled with tallow and lard from the animals. The land was flat now and seemingly endless. It was not nearly as hot as when they traversed the plains earlier in the year. Still, the heat waves rose from the scant grass and sandy soil. The season was well advanced into fall, and the grass was brown and dry. Angus discussed the varying plant life with Tom Pulaski, who seemed much more knowledgeable about the trail than him. Any variation spooked the horses and mules, and the overall dry grass was a nuisance to all the groups. The colonel warned the parties to be extra careful of the fire danger.

At the encampment that night, the sky was a lovely sight, drenched in reds of several sheens: dark pink, deep scarlet and crimson, gold and silver, bronze and gray. It was ever changing, the clouds parting and coming together in different shapes; Elmira gazed with wonder and pointed with glee for Lucas to enjoy the sight with her.

Elmira was popular with the men, and she and her husband spent time with the officers, while Angus sat with either the drivers or enlisted men. She ignored their crude manners and foul language on each occasion. She laughed at their jokes and sighed over their troubles. After the first week, she changed from her black, heavy garments to lighter, prettier gingham and calico. She wore an old bonnet with a wide brim to keep the sun from her eyes and pale face. She walked on most days, taking the boy with her, showing him unusually shaped rocks and pointing to birds and animals as they passed the time. At night, they sat hunched over the tablet with pencils in hand, until the boy grew sleepy. She sang as they rode on the wagon, and she told stories by the dozen. Tom seemed amused by her interest in the boy. He sometimes joined in, and even Juan took an interest on occasion.

When alone, with the lad asleep, she, Tom and Angus told of each other's backgrounds, but never did he tell of what he had heard about Adam Griswold. He was leaving that to discuss with Sheriff Terrill. He, instead, told her of his late wife, whom he had dearly loved, and who had died in his arms of a fever. He spoke of the boy, just past two years, who had drowned in a creek in Arkansas Territory. It was recalled with a sorrow he couldn't control. He revealed he was determined he wouldn't lose Lucas if it was within his power to protect him. Elmira comforted him and told of the two babies she had lost at birth. Then, she brightened and told of the three girls who had survived.

She was looking forward to seeing her grandchildren in Missouri. Tom laughed at her motherly nature and told her the grandchildren wouldn't know her, having been born since their excursion into Mexico.

It was on a lovely warm day, when they were passing between huge boulders near the mouth of a shallow canyon, that the bandits attacked. The army scouts raced for the wagons to warn them, but the caravan was strung out so long, in single formation, that it was impossible to save everyone. The lead company of Dragoons made it through the canyon, and Angus, Claymore and the other army wagons rolled out onto the open plains, but the Mexican traders and civilians were trapped. The sound of weapons firing echoed through the walls of the canyon, and Angus told Elmira to get in the back of the wagon as they circled with part of the Dragoons poised to guard them. He told the boy to hide under the seat. Juan pulled the carriage into a space near them. Tom hunkered down as best he could in the open carriage. They all grabbed weapons, ready to fight if necessary.

Half of the troops went back to help the other company and the civilians. The firing seemed to go on for hours, and Elmira prayed for the safety of the men. Angus argued that the bandits must have known they were coming and cursed the informer who had leaked the information. He sat on the seat with his flintlock in hand, the reins ready to hand if the order came to move out. Elmira started singing tenderly to Lucas in her soft contralto voice, and she began a story from the Bible.

Lucas gave a muffled laugh, and Angus bowed his head, sending up a few lengthy prayers of his own. Juan and Tom carried on a conversation through it all, while huddled in the carriage.

Finally, the sound of gunshots tapered off, and it became quiet in the canyon. Buzzards began to circle the area, riding the thermals and half-shaded by gray clouds, which turned out to be smoke, Angus heard later from Claymore and Captain Zolcroft. Still, the Dragoons and the army drivers waited, ready for trouble. A single horseman appeared, rode past Angus and met with an officer. The battle was over, but the toll on human lives was severe. They moved forward until all the surviving wagons and riders were safely out of the canyon. The Army surgeon and his assistant were kept busy for hours tending the wounded, and graves were dug beside the trail. Angus wanted to do something to help but was told to stay with his wagon; the supplies and ammunition in the wagon were more important than an extra hand with the work.

Elmira and Lucas came from the back, and Angus said it was safe to climb to the ground. Tom and Juan Cortez joined them, and they stood in a tiny circle, with Angus sitting high on his seat. Elmira walked to the wagon with the boy and dipped some water from the barrel for him to drink. She took a drink herself and brought some for Angus, for which he gratefully thanked her. Behind him, the civilian wagons came up, and they made a wide circle for protection, surrounded by Dragoons with their carbines and muskets ready.

The cook set up his tent and began to prepare a meal. Angus chaffed at the inactivity; all around him men were working or guarding or digging or helping in the hospital, but he sat like a lump of coal, doing nothing. He complained to a sergeant but was gruffly told to obey orders.

The sun began to sink into the horizon, and a faint breeze brought the smell of death. Smoke filled the sky; and still Angus sat on his wagon seat, the boy and Elmira beside him. Juan and Tom walked a while then sat in the carriage. Finally, a private rode down the line telling the men they could relax and eat their meal; first the Dragoon officers not on duty, then the privates and sergeants. Next, the drivers could take their place in line, and Angus secured the reins and climbed from his wagon. It had been a long, frustrating day, and he worked out the stiffness in his arms and legs. He circled the wagon to help Elmira and the boy down. She joined her husband, and Angus took the hand of the boy in his rough, calloused one and smiled at him. They stood in line to receive their portion of the quickly cooked stew and bread. Lucas smiled to see fried apple fritters for desert. A cook's helper gave them a cup of coffee, and they moved to sit with the other people. Several of the civilian freighters were sitting with bandages on heads or arms and displaying a shocked look in their eyes. Tom Pulaski went down the line, talking to his fellow traders and giving them comfort when he could. Juan sat with some Mexican servants, where he could converse in his native language.

They ate without speaking. When she finished, Elmira went to the women and asked if she could help. The people were joined in solidarity against a common enemy, the bandits. Gossip flew through the camp of atrocities and heroism. Angus decided that Lucas didn't need to hear of the violence, so he went back to the wagon and, when told it was safe, dug a pit, built a fire and set up his tent for the night. All the while, he talked softly to the boy and instructed him on how he could help.

Elmira returned to the wagon, but she only smiled at the boy and began to teach him the next letter in the alphabet. She and Angus exchanged glances, but it wasn't time to discuss the day's events. They didn't want the boy to hear of the wagon train's travail.

Just as the sun was perched to fall below the horizon, the colonel rode on his stout brown horse throughout the camp, stopping to speak to each group, and passing on to the next. It somehow lent an author-ity and unity to the encampment. At last darkness fell over the scene of disaster. After seeing that Lucas was inside the tent and comfortable, Angus and Tom walked to Claymore's tent and in whispers of dismay and despair learned some of the details of the battle. Five dead, six severely wounded, two wagons stolen along with their mules and contents. It could have been a lot worse, except for the bravery of the Dragoons at the rear of the caravan and the skill of the surgeon and his helpers.

— 10 —

They remained in camp for three days, until some of the worst of the wounded could be moved; during the time, clothing and bedding were washed; water barrels filled; animals tended to; and the account of the battle was discussed and debated. Among the charges, they argued about who was responsible for the disaster.

On the morning of the fourth day, in a soft mist, the caravan again spread out across the prairie. Nerves were strained, and exhaustion settled among the soldiers and drivers alike; a few fights broke out among the men. Through it all, Elmira Pulaski kept a cheerful countenance, sang and told amusing stories to Lucas and Angus. Her eyes sparkled with life and love for the boy in her care. Her husband supported her, and Angus remarked on her bravery and endurance. At last the caravan pulled in near the last river crossing, and she began to seem more melancholy and solemn. He asked her what the matter could be, and she confessed she would miss the boy and him. She and Tom would be happy to see their daughters and grandchildren, but the weeks spent with them had given her a new and enduring look at life.

Angus felt the same way and told her so. She had brought them through the grief and the sorrow of the long journey from Santa Fe, and he would remember her always. The road across the country had been and would continue to be monotonous. The heat sent wavy lines across the horizon and sometimes produced a mirage, tall castles as in medieval times or lakes of crystal water in the air. Driving a wagon across the plains, even surrounded by strong, valiant men, gave one a sense of isolation, and if it hadn't been for the woman's cheerful attitude and the cherished hope for the future of his son, Angus Meldrick shared privately that he wasn't sure he would have made it back to Missouri. Even so, they crossed the boundary, and the clear flowing streams, the huge towering trees and singing birds were welcome sights to the vagabonds. The journey from Independence to Jefferson Barracks was a flight of fancy in comparison to the long trek through the mountains and across the plains.

The gates of Jefferson Barracks opened wide, and the veterans of the trek to Santa Fe rode in to the accompaniment of the brass band. Greetings were exchanged, and the supplies were removed from the wagons and stacked in warehouses prepared for their return. Tom made plans at a hotel for himself and his wife and sent off letters to his daughters that they were on their way home. He and Elmira were invited to stay with a sergeant and his wife and children while they were at the Barracks waiting for transport to their daughter's home. The hospital wagon was parked in its place near the hospital building. The cooks and bakers put away their ovens and stoves; and Angus drove his wagon to the door of the warehouse and reported to the officer of the day; he and the boy took up residence again in his two rooms near the blacksmith's forge.

He took care of his personal business, put his belongings away and asked Elmira to watch the boy for a few hours. At her nod of agreement, he borrowed a horse from the friendly blacksmith and rode into town. He stopped at Slim's saloon, where he was welcomed with a joyful shout from his friends. He bought a drink, swallowed it quickly and asked if anyone knew where the sheriff might be at that time of day. Told he had last been seen in his office, he left the saloon and headed that way, his stride long and determined. He was stopped by several townspeople who knew him by sight and asked about his latest trip. He replied politely, although without giving away any details. One lady holding a large umbrella asked after the boy, and Angus was surprised that someone had remembered.

There had been a slight mist, at first just enough to settle the dust, when he left the fort, but now the rain had strengthened into a torrent, and he splashed in the puddles as he crossed to the building displaying the sign with large blocked letters across the portal that proclaimed Sheriff. He opened the door, stepped inside and removed his dripping hat, making a puddle on the floor when he dropped it.

The sheriff looked up, a frown on his brow, when the door to his office opened without ceremony. The frown broke into a smile when he saw the man coming in but wavered when he saw the gleam in Angus Meldrick's eyes. He rose from his chair and came around to shake hands.

"Why didn't you tell me there was an inquest into Griswold's death? I was still at the Barracks. I could have come to town to see for myself the witnesses and hear their testimony." Angus refused the hand held out to him, and the sheriff dropped it to his side.

"How did you find out? Angus, I didn't think you needed to hear the gory details, what with your taking charge of the boy so soon after the victim's death. Where is the boy?" Wade Terrill's face had grown pale, and his eyes reflected his regret over the outcome of the judge's decision. Angus crumpled like a marionette. He found the nearest chair, which happened to be in front of the desk, and sat down. He blew out his cheeks, his anger suddenly gone.

"The boy's fine. He's with his teacher and companion at the Barracks."

"Really? A teacher for the boy? How did that come about?" Terrill pulled up a secondary chair and sat with his elbows resting on his knees, watching Angus' face intently.

Angus nodded and looked around the office to keep his emotions from showing. "A charming lady and her husband, one of the Mexican traders, were stranded in Santa Fe, and we traveled together to Missouri. They're waiting to hear from their daughter before leaving for their home. A nice couple; very kind, and the boy will miss them. Name's Pulaski; you might have heard of them; he's from Poland?" But the sheriff shook his head to indicate that he didn't know the couple.

Angus grew serious. "Tell me about the inquest again and why you didn't invite me to attend. Did you think I wouldn't be interested in how my boy's father died? By the way, where is Lily? I didn't see her just now at Slim's bar."

Terrill smiled. "It's good to hear you refer to him as your son. It seems you've grown attached. He's got no one else, so if there's to be a father for him, it seems you're it."

"Yeah, you could say that. I appreciate your sentiments. About Lily?"

"She left town soon after you did. The gossip wouldn't die down. Some people still speak of it even though it's been several months now. How did you find out about the inquest?"

"Ran into a man named Simmons at the alcalde's house in Santa Fe. Do you remember him? One of the merchants headed to Chihuahua. His wife started it off. She said he was a witness to the killing at the inquest." He watched the expressions cross his old friend's face.

"I remember Simmons. He confirmed what Judge Maddock and the sergeant, Palmer, his name is, said about the shooting. Griswold got caught in the crossfire when Garland went for his gun against Langston. Several other men have come forward since the inquest. Griswold had found a room in a boarding house for his aunt and the child and was apparently planning to keep him there until he could get accommodations at the Barracks. The landlady confirmed he paid a month in advance. She gave it to me. I suppose it belongs to you, now." He opened his drawer, removed a few bills and handed them to Angus. Angus hesitated to take the money, saying it felt like payment for a man's death, but in the end, the sheriff said it could be used for the boy's education, and he didn't refuse.

He sat back down. "The case is settled, now? Griswold has been cleared of any assignation with Lily? For the boy, this is important. One day he'll have to be told how his father died. Griswold was a fool for leaving his family behind in Natchez, but he wasn't a cad."

"I agree with you." Terrill continued that Angus could be assured that Griswold was ready to take responsibility for his son when his wife died, by all accounts that he'd been able to ascertain. "There's one more thing, my friend."

"Yes, Wade? I'm sorry. It's been a long trip. Is the case settled, then?" Angus yawned, unable to fight the tiredness and growing sleepiness left by the final days of the trip.

"Yes. Garland was caught cheating again in Liberty, Missouri, across from Fort Leavenworth. He was killed by the town marshal when he tried to steal a horse and ride out of town."

"Killed? Garland is dead, too? Wade, are you sure?" At first excited, Angus's enthusiasm evaporated as quickly as it had come, and he shrugged his shoulders. "I don't suppose it matters. Certainly not to Lucas; he's so young, but what'll I tell the boy about his father when he grows up? Can I tell him that he was accidently shot in a bar? I wouldn't want to hear that about my father, if it were true."

"Tell the boy whatever you think best. There's no stopping the rumors about Lily, but maybe the gossip will fade in time. How is the boy? Are you going to keep him? I never pictured you as the fathering type, though you shouldn't make anything of that. Sometimes fathering comes with the opportunity, not with just wishing for it. You've always been steadfast, probably the best quality for raising a boy."

"Of course, I'll keep him. He's my son, and I love him as if he's my own. I need to find a school or a tutor; a boarding school, maybe, for when I'm away on these long trips, but I'm going to find Judge Maddock and see about making it permanent. Adopt him legally." Angus stood up as though the interview was over. "Thank you for the information, Wade. I'll see you around."

Angus left the sheriff's office with a satisfied

expression on his face. The rain had stopped, leaving a sweet, fresh fragrance in the air. A few patchy blue spots could be seen among the clouds, high above the roofs of the buildings. He sighed and stepped around a puddle as he walked to the Hash House, where he ordered a big steak, potatoes and onions from Majesty when she came to take his order. He renewed his acquaintance with several people in the restaurant and returned to his quarters. He was in a better mood but exhausted as he took off his boots, pants and shirt and slept for an hour.

He rose, washed his face, combed his hair and went to pick up his son. The sun was now shining bright and yellow in the western sky. The warmth burned into his face and neck. He stayed for a few minutes talking to Elmira and the sergeant's wife and took his son home.

— 11 —

The weeks seemed to creep along after the excitement of the trip to Santa Fe. Tom and Elmira received a note from their daughter and were soon on a stage coach headed northward. Angus and Lucas watched them go, their affection for her clear for all to see. Juan left with another wagon train bound for Mexico.

Being stationed at the Barracks between assignments was the hard part; driving a wagon was an easy task; it was the inactivity, the boredom of Barracks life that chafed at Angus' soul. He wasn't alone in this. All the soldiers who weren't on duty sat around, playing cards, attending or participating in wrestling matches, reading books or playing board games. Captain Nelson, who'd been polite but distant and formal to Angus during the campaign to Santa Fe, made the rounds of the Barracks by horseback and foot. His impeccable attire and precise and predictable inspections seemed to keep the men on their toes, but privately, only when he was in their presence. Horseshoes was a popular game among the troopers, and Angus joined them when he felt like doing something active. The laughter and shouts of the men were as common as the sound of the bugle at morning and night, calling them to meals, to duty or to rest. The Sunday afternoon horse races became a source of entertainment for Lucas as he waved his wooden horse in the air and shouted with the adults. He named it Brownie, and Angus never knew why.

He took Lucas for long walks around the grounds, visited the bakers for a hot cross bun or small iced cakes. They watched the smithy at work, and Angus was offered a job as helper; he was good at shoeing horses. He accepted and spent a few hours each day at the forge or in the stables with the horses and mules. At night Lucas finished learning the alphabet and started forming simple words on his tablet with his pencils. The two primer books Angus had found helped him keep a schedule, and the boy learned quickly. He played with his slingshot until he killed a stray cat that had wandered onto the parade grounds, and Angus took it from him. Lucas found a limb and started waving it about as a sword like the officers.

A large contingency of raw recruits enlisted and started training. It was entertaining to watch those who weren't familiar with horses learning to ride, jump hurdles and practice with their weapons. Lucas, especially, seemed fascinated by the exercise, and Angus often missed him from the rooms they shared and found he had sneaked away to watch the men. He hadn't the heart to punish him, but cautioned him to always tell him where he was going.

Among these recruits was a strapping young man named James Biltmore, who seemed to take a liking to Lucas and came to visit at night after mess. He had brown hair and eyes and came from New Jersey. He was now two and twenty, and barely had enough hair on his chin to shave. Angus discovered the man was lonely like himself, and they enjoyed many a night talking and playing a friendly game of poker after Lucas was asleep. He volunteered to stay with Lucas whenever Angus felt the need to go into town, if he wasn't on duty himself.

The relationship was a good one for both men, and the events that happened one winter evening solidified their friendship for life. Angus discovered, after a pint of stout down Biltmore's gullet, that the man had a strong aversion to birthday celebrations, so he had no choice but to harangue him when he learned he was prepared to let his celebratory day pass without fanfare. In secret, so Biltmore would be unaware, Angus passed the hat for a minor gift – a leather belt engraved with the man's name – and got several of the soldier's company to join him before their evening game of poker. The camp cook had prepared a small cake for the occasion, and Angus had it on a low sideboard, covered so that it would be unnoticed. The occasion was to be a pretend confrontation between the soldiers and Angus. They would burst from the door just as Biltmore arrived, only revealing their plot when the man became confused at the scene.

The gaffe came when Biltmore became enraged and pulled out his revolver. He wrestled Angus free, even as his fellow soldiers fell away laughing, and pulled him roughly into Angus' quarters, accidentally knocking over the oil lamp onto the horsehair sofa and setting it alight. There was a scramble to put out the flames. Poor Biltmore was in disarray for a time, and his eyes smoldered, but he eventually eased into the joke, and the shared birthday confection sweetened the evening. The unexpected buffoonery and the singed sofa became a jest that the men in the Barracks teased Biltmore about from that day forward, giving him the nickname Blazing Biltmore.

The young soldier had experienced no trouble adjusting to army life, he once shared with Angus. He had learned to ride horses at an early age, and guns and their maintenance were second nature to him. Many nights, after their poker game, they would disassemble and clean Army weaponry, until even Angus could do so with his eyes closed. Biltmore assured the freighter that the skill would come in useful to him, even if he couldn't see the importance of it at the time.

The weather turned cold and damp; fall brought an epidemic of influenza, and the surgeon and his helpers were kept busy in the hospital barracks; two men died and several officers were forced to resign their commission from weakness and a prolonged cough and lung congestion. One day, as Angus was dressing the boy to go outside, he remarked that he was glad he'd decided in Santa Fe to buy Lucas a heavy winter coat. Lucas held out his hands to show that the sleeves had grown too short for his arms. Angus smiled and said he hoped it would last until spring. He pulled at the boy's legs and said it was the trousers that seemed to be shrinking each month; the boy was almost to Angus' armpits, and he knew the lad would be tall when finished growing.

Angus talked to Judge Maddock, and the papers were signed and sealed giving him the rights of guardianship over the minor child, Lucas Wayne Griswold. His name was legally changed to Meldrick. The townspeople became accustomed to seeing the tall freight driver and his son on the streets of the city. They were equally welcome in the quarters of the Dragoons at Jefferson Barracks. He wrote to Elmira the happy news of the adoption, and she replied that she was pleased and would like to see them again, but she was busy with her grandchildren. She sent them a tintype of herself with a big smile on her face.

It was a bad winter. Snow seemed to be constantly on the ground, and when it wasn't, the days were gray and gloomy. Christmas was celebrated with restraint and sobriety, as one of the older and well-liked captains had died the night before. He was buried with full military honors in the graveyard, and all who knew him mourned. Letters of condolence were sent to the fam-

164

ily, and many signed them, including Angus and young Biltmore.

One evening, Angus remarked to his friend Biltmore that increasingly more Dragoon companies were being transferred to Fort Leavenworth, and one bright, crisp day in March, the company of Lieutenant Frederick Packard and his men rode away, their banners and flags flapping in the breeze. He had seen the lieutenant often on the grounds or at the mess hall eating, but they hadn't come into contact. It was better that way, he supposed. Among Lieutenant Selwig's former company was Private Zellers. He had watched over the boy many times, and they had become friendly; Angus wished him well and told him Lucas was dismayed to see him go.

Angus was assigned wood-gathering details into the forests, trips into St. Louis to pick up supplies at the shipping wharfs, long monotonous trips to far-flung destinations, or short dispatch trips to the other forts; on his dispatch trips, he was seen riding a horse, not driving a wagon. He finally admitted it was time to find a more permanent setting for Lucas. The privates were helpful in caring for him at short notice, but they had their own careers at stake.

With the help of the judge and the sheriff as character references, Angus found a boarding school that was highly recommended for the boy. He took up residence under the name Lucas Wayne Meldrick. He balked at first, but when Angus explained about his job, the boy was able to remember enough of the trip to understand that he couldn't keep him at the Barracks. After a few weeks, he joined happily in the scholarly fellowship of the school and was popular with the teachers and students alike.

Rumors were building daily, fed by the weekly newspaper accounts of atrocities in the South. Army dispatches arrived, revealing military buildups in key locations. Many of the men arriving were fresh recruits who had swarmed to recruitment centers to join in the war effort, anxious not to be left out. Angus discussed with Biltmore the alcalde of Santa Fe and the other people he had met at the dinner in the great hall of the local government. He told of Dona Maria Fortunado and wondered if war was declared, if she or her husband and children would be sucked into the politics of aggression against the States. Biltmore agreed that it was possible, but the young man was eager to join his comrades in battle. Angus opined that he hoped it wouldn't come to that, but as spring came, there was little doubt among the military that hostilities would soon be declared.

"Angus, we can't let those heathens run us out of the territories. Since the annexation of Texas, the bandits and Indian raiders have grown more daring and dangerous. I've got to get my hand in before long. Some of my friends think it'll be war soon." Biltmore paced the room, and his face glowed with the anticipation of his first engagement with an enemy.

"James, it's not all glory and honor and nobility. It's death and disease; and many will be maimed and property will be destroyed." Angus shook his head but didn't say more.

And, so it was. War was declared in May of 1846, and James Biltmore was one of the first soldiers that rode away from the Barracks to replace men from Fort Leavenworth who would be traveling the old route to Santa Fe and to California. Angus haunted the adjutant's and the quartermaster's offices, but was told again and again that he wouldn't be making the trip. In the end, it was Claymore who was sent out in the lead supply wagon to join with the men forming at Leavenworth, and Angus was saddened to see him go. They had been on many trails together. Alterson and young Hawthorne went as drivers of the other wagons. The cook and the surgeon remained at Jefferson Barracks, while unknown company cooks and surgeons were sent from Leavenworth.

The war dragged on, and Angus continued his job in supply duty, or as dispatcher between Jefferson and Leavenworth. He grew so accustomed to the road trip that he could travel it in the dark, which he often did. He was a lone rider on horseback, racing with important letters and documents in his saddlebags, his face haggard and his body weary. He scrutinized with dread the newspapers left on the steamers from New Orleans. He watched with frustration as the Barracks became a major supply depot and training ground. New recruits were joining every month, only to be sent elsewhere when they finished training. The news was increasingly bad; names of Mexican towns and villages were spoken in whispers or shouts of triumph: San Jacinto, Los Angeles, Tabasco, Veracruz, Pueblo; and finally, a weary country celebrated the treaty signed at Guadalupe Hidalgo in February of 1848.

Angus learned of the end of the war not at the Barracks, but in St. Louis. Having stopped at the steamboat pier to pick up cargo to transport to the fort, he pulled his mules up and dropped from his wagon. He and two other fellows began to load the heavy crates and numerous bags of corn and flour that had arrived for the Barracks into his wagon, when they heard the loud sound of a cheering crowd coming down the street. Dust swirled at their feet, and a couple of the participants seemed to have already indulged in a celebratory drink or two. As their words grew louder, their meaning became clear. The war was over. Angus was bewildered and half disbelieving as his two helpers joined the crowd and surrounded him, jostling, with much hand-shaking and offers of free smokes to anyone who wanted one before passing on down the street, leaving him alone on the platform.

He walked to the agent's window and Casey thrust a paper through the bars.

"Read this, Angus. It just come up from New Orleans. Might drive some of us out of a job. Then maybe not, as there's always people needing packages and barrels delivered, ya' know."

Angus laid open the newspaper to see the banner across the top, announcing the successful completion of the wartime activities. He smiled at Casey, and in his usual taciturn way, tucked the printed tome under his arm to read later, and finished loading the supplies into his wagon. He could hear the sound of the crowds cheering in the city as he drove away from the wharf. As soon as he could, he stopped the vehicle and read the article headlined in the newspaper before driving on. A group of Dragoons passed him heading toward town, and he waved at them.

Lieutenant Ben Lacy of G Company stopped to greet him, allowing his fellow troopers to ride on.

"Did you hear the news, Angus? It's all over; the shooting and the killing." He had a broad grin on his face.

"Yeh, I heard. This just came up on the steamer, Casey at the wharf said," and he handed the paper to Lacy, who leaned from his horse to receive it. The horse blew air from his nostrils and shifted his weight, as the soldier opened the paper. The lieutenant gazed up at Angus with a pleased smile.

"This confirms the news, then. I'll share it with the boys when I get to town. Much obliged, Angus." And he rode away, a loud shout coming from his mouth.

Angus laughed and clucked to his mules. When he was certain the Dragoon was far enough away from him, he gave a loud shout himself and started singing an old Army tune, only slightly off-key.

There was a more personal day connected with the end of the war when Lucas and Angus happened to meet up with Biltmore and several of Biltmore's army chums who returned from the war effort flush with their success, even as their uniforms were caked with the dust of the trail and the soil of many nights spent under the stars. Angus and the boy stood on the wharf, having arrived to pick up some sundries and other cargo, when the Army troops began to disembark the boat.

"Papa, soldiers!" Lucas, having grown over the years the war had raged on, was nearly as tall as Angus and able to look him in the eyes. "The war is truly over, then? All the men are coming home?"

About then, Biltmore stepped down the ramp, and his face brightened as he called to his old friend. "Angus, you buzzard! I see your son's with you. He must be eating well, as his arms and legs have out-grown the rest of him."

"Son, what do you think?" Angus clapped the sea-soned veteran on the shoulder as the man threw his arms around him in an enthusiastic greeting. "Blazing Biltmore has returned to finish burning my sofa to the ground."

"Ah, will I never live that down?" Biltmore laughed, and as several of his friends had gathered to listen, he leaned in to Lucas and whispered, "It was a stinky sofa, to be sure, and it deserved to be set on fire."

Two years it had taken, and it was over at last. Around drinks at Slim's saloon, Biltmore and his com-panions told Angus and Lucas of dozens of Dragoons and infantry that were killed and wounded. Towns and farms had been destroyed, as Angus had predicted so many months ago. The end of the war was celebrated with military parades, their banners and flags flying in the afternoon breeze, with church bells, steamboat whistles and political speeches from the steps of the State Capitol. Angus and Lucas agreed to travel with Biltmore's company to see it all, spending the night in a crowded hotel as a treat to celebrate the ending of the war.

Throughout the festivities, there was a jovial air, with people laughing, families walking the streets, and food peddlers at every corner. Red, white and blue banners sprouted on every building, flashing in the sun as the wind whipped them to and fro. Angus Meldrick took it all in and shook his head at the hypocrisy and vanity of mankind. He slept soundly that night for the first time in months.

— Epilogue —

Angus Meldrick continued to drive the freight wagon while his son was attending school. Lucas Wayne Meldrick grew up to be a soldier as his birth father once was. He attended the West Point Academy, graduating an officer at the top of his class. He fought proudly for the Army of the Potomac under General Hooker in the War of the Rebellion and was decorated for his outstanding valor at Chancellorsville, in Virginia. He married Bonita Evangelista, of Mexican descent, and fathered four children, three girls and one son, who became a Tennessee senator and respected merchant.

Angus made two more trips to Santa Fe, now a part of the United States. When Lucas was transferred to a post on the western frontier, Angus followed him and supported himself as a harness repairman, until his calloused hands became stiff and unresponsive. He was a familiar sight among the young recruits and the seasoned veterans with his white hair and quiet manner. If sometimes his mind wandered to the days on the Santa Fe Trail and the battle at the canyon, they passed it off as the vagrancies of old age.

With his final transfer, Lucas made his home among the adobe structures of New Mexico. Angus, now into his fifties, with his son married and settled in Santa Fe, retired and took a job as helper in a blacksmith's shop and enjoyed the antics of his grandchildren.

Lucas supported the American government and took his place in city management, to ensure the rights and safety of all nationalities and cultures under the protection of the United States Army. During a government-sanctioned trip to Memphis in the summer of 1878, he, his wife and one daughter succumbed to the yellow fever plague that killed over 5,000 in the city that year. Due to his long association with the military, he received a military burial with full honors befitting the life of such an outstanding citizen. Lucas's son remained in Tennessee at the Church Home orphanage with his two surviving sisters, where Franklin Meldrick received his inspiration to enter politics at an early age.

On a cold, silent winter night with snow on the ground, the old freighter was found dead in his sleep. His neighbors were surprised when they went through his possessions to find the daguerreotypes of Lieutenant Adam Griswold and his wife and son. Several military markings of rank and other identification were discovered on the backs, and a local historian was charged to research the name and background of the unknown man for their military archives. His last post was found to be Jefferson Barracks, in Missouri. The researcher discovered his stone in the post cemetery. After months of speculation and research, a conclusion was reached. Lieutenant Adam Griswold had been killed in the line of duty, and his name was chiseled into the memorial wall of the honored dead. There was no one alive to dispute the record, and the graves of his wife and son were never found.

www.ingramcontent.com/pod-product-compliance
Lightning Source LLC
Chambersburg PA
CBHW071248130626
46556CB00003B/1214